Copyright For Linton Robinson
By Publisher: Adoro Books
Baja California
2013

AdoroBooks.com

CONTENTS

CHAPTER ONE

You've seen those banks so old and fusty they still have gilded wrought iron cages for the tellers. Walnut paneling and mahogany waste baskets. Some drowsing, grey-haired security guard looking like he rode with the Earps. Bulgy old Rixler vault with a big gold wheel. Spittoons, maybe even. You get 'em in dried up little Texas towns. The lobby said as much about the financial and social conditions of Chisolm County as any disparaging audit could have implied. You expect a wire haired old banker in bifocals, vest, and sleeve garters to walk out of the frosted glass door to his den-like office any moment, comforting and sagely advising the widow of a big rancher. Maybe even some duster-clad owlhoots to bust on in, breathing through bandanas and waving hogleg six guns. Matt and Maverick and Miss Kitty setting up a Christmas club.

Well, times change, even though a lot of tumbleweed Texas towns don't get around to it. Closest you're gonna get today is Cole Haskins walking in and heading right up to the teller cage with the dust-mummied hundred year-old lady wearing navy crepe with a few ink smudges. Cutting right in front of the line like some back pasture honyock, and this on a Monday, mind you.

A few of the ladies in line didn't seem to mind Cole getting ahead of himself, because he was pretty easy on the eyes. A slightly urbanized cowboy, for all his scuffed boots and rope calluses: brave, young and handsome. His incursion into the rightful order of things earned him a bushy-browed dirty look from the old bat in the moldy teller cave, and she didn't lay it off any when he hit her with his sundowner grin. She was too offended to even speak when Cole sidled up to Carl, the local saloon owner, who was fixing to make his deposit. And bold as brass said, "Scuse me, cousin, can I cut through here? Bit of a hurry."

That loosened her tongue and waspish old attitude, for sure. "Please wait your, turn, sir." Butter wouldn't have melted off that "Sir", even in August.

The barkeep looked up from writing the slip for the cash the roughnecks and cowhands had flushed him with all weekend and frowned slightly. "Hold your horses, pal. I'm right in the middle of something."

"I just can't see as it matters much, frankly." Cole tipped his crimped-brim Stetson to the scowling teller. "This being a stick-up and all."

The teller gasped and quailed back from the window. The guard, more alert than he looked, came up out of his chair, slapping leather. But Cole whirled, brushing back his jacket in a Sundance move and whipping out a big Bisley grip revolver with shocking speed. That guard had been around in his younger day and knew The Drop when he saw it. He came out of his crouch, raising both hands. Cole motioned almost graciously with the big .45. "Just toss your pistol over in that planter, there, if you like."

The guard complied without visible emotional reaction, keeping his hands in sight. Cole turned to the two frozen tellers, the bald septuagenarian in gold wire rims and real cufflinks as petrified as the old bat. Cole gave them another aw shucks grin, but they didn't show any sign of warming up, so he waved the hefty handgun again and told them, "Can't think of nothing original, so just, you know... put the cash in a nice sturdy bag." The chrome-dome unfroze first, pulled out a canvas money sack and started stuffing it with greenbacks.

2

Cole turned to the wide-eyed customers, sweeping off his hat like a Confederate cavalryman, his sun-blonde hair spilling down around his ears. "And if ya'll could just drop your valuables right there in John Stetson, that'd do just fine."

He did a pass down both lines, getting watches and wallets. When the street door clicked, he was covering it before it even opened, then had to give another barrel wave to get the slicker in a western suit and turquoise bolo tie to close it behind him. The man was calf-eyed in front of the gun, strongly suspected of having just wet his pants. Cole had to walk over to collect his wallet and pocket watch, almost had to haul the bolo off him. Leaving only the bar owner, who had his arms wrapped around his leather zip bag of banknotes and was looking not so much stubborn as just plain locked-up.

Amused, Cole gestured with the revolver, starting to run short of movie flourishes to get these heifers to comply. The barman tightened his grip, shaking his head woodenly. Cole sighed, tipped the hat full of loot back on his head, and stepped over to the cage to hold the muzzle of the Colt to the guy's nose while dragging the case out of his clutches. He let it fall open, and whistled appreciatively at one great big passel of cash.

Coming to grips with his loss, the businessman muttered ruefully, "More in there than you're rakin' from the bank, Hoss."

"Looks like it from here," Cole affably agreed.

"Don't suppose you'd let me finish my deposit?" the publican said without a whole lot of hope. "I was first in line, after all."

His surprise was evident when Cole drawled, "Okay, cousin, but make it snappy, will you?"

Oozing relief, he gave a weak smile. "I've got my slip made out and everything."

The granny teller dumped a till into a plastic trash bag, knotted the top and pushed it over the counter at Cole, who nodded at his victim. Who quickly handed over his deposit slip.

A robbery was one thing, but blatant violation of bank policy steeled the old nanny. "Sir, we can't possibly accept..."

Cole grabbed the bag and pointed his gun right in her face. "Accentuate the possible, my mama used to say."

Shuddering, the teller took the slip, hit register keys, and handed out a receipt. The businessman handed her the clutch full of bills and Cole immediately took it back. "There ya go. Now it's just between you and him and the FDI of C."

Backing towards the door with the money case under his left arm and the trash bag in the same hand, Cole touched his hat brim with his gun hand. "Many thanks to each and all, and a fond adios."

Anybody who thought the bank lobby looked antiquated, dusty, and sleep-ridden would have been further rewarded by the street outside. A somnolent desert burg dreaming of attaining ghost town status, it evoked bygone TV westerns with its old-fashioned glass storefronts and second story false fronts, broken only by a few dark brick edifices once fine and proud enough to rate dates on their curved granite keystones.

The only activity was a desultory argument between two grade school boys at the main corner, the larger dominating a tussle over a beaten skateboard. The argument was pacified by the

4

arrival of a fifteen year-old patrol car, the boys hiding their hands and averting their eyes as a weary-looking cop in his fifties got out and confronted them. As soon as he started his kindly interrogation, both kids produced fingers, each pointed at the other.

Excitement enough for this little hamlet, but it was immediately eclipsed when Cole stepped out of the bank at the next corner; carrying a trash bag, the leather money case, and a big old shooting iron. The cop reacted at once, grabbing the two kids--scaring the hell out of them since they had not seen Cole, just a police officer snatching them up--and shoving them into the shelter of the corner.

The driver's door of the cruiser slammed open at once, a stocky officer in his late twenties popping out; shouting into a microphone in one hand while the other hand swung a shotgun over the roof of the car. Sheltered by the corner of the brick dry goods store, the older cop also pulled his sidearm, thrilling the two brats to the point of jumping up and down with their fists in their mouths.

Hearing the rasp of the shotgun's pump, Cole stepped between two diagonal-parked cars and laid his gun over the hood of one. He was sighting in, sizing up, and awaiting the next move when the trash bag in his hand exploded into a splashy burst of green bills and orange dye. Simultaneously an old domed iron alarm bell on the bank's façade started a truly obnoxious clamor. Sirens could be heard nearby, and getting even nearer by.

Holding the gun pointed, sprayed with sticky international orange dye, Cole gaped at the money spilled all over the street. The omnipresent West Texas wind blew it down the street, fluttering into drifts along the face of the bank. Opening the money

5

clutch, he started grabbing money off the sidewalk with his gun hand and stuffing it into the slit opening in the bag.

Down the block, the younger cop fired a warning shotgun blast. Cole snapped erect and popped off a quick shot that hit the shotgun, almost a block away, right in the receiver, bashing it out of the cop's hands. The older cop stared in wonder at the shot, then returned fire as another squad car pulled in at the near corner, two backup cops jumping out to draw down on Cole. Who kept on grabbing money up and stuffing it into the case and his pockets. He continued down the sidewalk, covering his movement with occasional snapshots at the Law, spooky quick and incredibly accurate. He snatched up more money from the orange-smeared piles in front of the bank.

He had just bluffed the backup cops into ducking behind their car with a fancy juke move when the front window of the bank blew out and he went down amid the sleet of old-fashioned violet glass pellets, hit twice and bleeding. The security guard stood inside the ruined window in a police academy shooting crouch, but when Cole rolled over and returned fire, he flattened out on the floor.

Cole rolled to his knees, groveling up more cash, but a solid hit by the younger cop toppled him against the front wall. He pushed himself along the wall, staggering in a stoop to shovel up more money in between pointing his gun at the cops. Hit in the thigh, he went down again. Moving like a striking rattler, he snapped off a shot that drove both the backup cops to dive behind their car, but there was no report. He had come up empty.

Struggling to his knees, he inched along the wall, fumbling for cash and pointing his pistols at the

6

cops. They ducked a few times more, then cautiously moved from cover, converging to surround Cole as he oozed along the wall, painting it with two streaks of blood as he scooped bills into his waistband.

All four officers approached Cole, pointing pistols at him with both hands, staring in disbelief as he grimly grabbed up cash, spinning shakily to point his gun first at one, then the other. They relaxed a little, glancing at each other in sheer amazement. What will it take for this hotshot to realize it's all over?

At which point an over-powered, chromium yellow, late model Mustang arrived somewhat spectacularly at the scene, bombing up onto the sidewalk to clip all four cops off their feet. It screeched to a stop, hurling the passenger door open right in front of the slumped Cole Haskins.

He lurched to the door, tossed in the clutch of money, and pulled himself painfully into the seat, smearing it with bright orange dye and dark red blood. He reached out for more of the money eddying in the prairie wind, and took a shot in the upper arm from inside the bank.

The driver of the car, a gorgeous, built and somewhat terrifying young brunette named Bunny Beaumont, leaned over from the wheel, pointed a large automatic pistol with extension magazine through the window and touched off a barrage that blasted out the remaining glass and eliminated further resistance. She screamed in a pronounced East Texas accent, "Get your feet in Cole! Get *in*, damn your sorry butt! *Cole!*"

Groaning, spurting blood from a half-dozen sites, Cole lugged his legs inside. Bunny immediately stomped on the gas and the car lunged down the sidewalk, the door slamming shut from sheer momentum.

At the corner, Bunny barreled the car off the curb, impacting and demolishing the disputed skateboard, and blasted noisily towards the classic Western escapade direction, Thataway. Behind her the two boys, now welded into eternal friendship by having mutually witnessed the bitchinest thing that ever happened in their nowhere little burg, celebrated it by chorusing, "AWESOME!"

Bunny, steady and steely-eyed when wheeling getaways, performing vehicular mayhem, and pot-shotting your occasional law officer, was losing it as she floored the car out the desolate stretch of two-lane blacktop leading significantly south. Fighting panic at the site of blood flowing copiously from Cole's various perforations, she waved her pistol like a conductor's baton, attempting to direct the movement towards Life and Light. "Don't you even think about dying on me, Cole Haskins," she yelled. "You make one dying move, I'll blow your damn head off. You hear me, Cole?"

Pale and hunched on the seat, smearing blood on the passenger window, Cole dragged his focus to the living world, and the yawing highway they were skimming along at over a hundred and thirty. "Watch your driving, Honeybunny. We don't need no accidents in this damn town. They're mean here."

"Shut up, Cole Haskins," Bunny bawled. "You die on me and I'll kill you within an inch of your no-good life!"

Cole moaned, not all his misery physical. "I can't believe I left all that money lying in the street."

"*Money?* The concept made her livid. "Money! *Damn* you, Cole!"

She hauled off to hit him with the gun but he coughed wetly, blood dribbling down his chin, and she dropped it onto the seat, her eyes wide and pained. She turned her attention to the road, pouring on even more speed, jabbering, "Shut up, Cole. Just shut up, shut up, shut up, shut up."

Cole nodded understandingly, said "Believe I will," and passed out, cash gripped in his fist.

Bunny bit her lip until it was also bleeding, leaning forward as she tore along the hardtop, racing in search of some kind of Plan B. When she passed a weathered four by four supporting a bullet-riddled sign proclaiming, LEAVING CHISOLM COUNTY, she whipped the wheel savagely to the right, the pitchpoling signpost giving the stolen Mustang the first scars and dents of its pampered existence.

CHAPTER TWO

If the bank in Chisolm represented a dismal prospectus, the offices inside the picturesque but decaying old post-Confederate City Hall of Sulfur Wells brought depressive assessments home to roost. Everything about the aged oak furnishings, outdated calendars, dusty paperwork, and tacky appointments suggested a city on the brink, if not actually nearing the point of some sordid little impact with fiscal disgrace and depopulation.

Ironically, the actual fiscal picture wasn't as bad as all that, and even more ironically, the forlorn hopes were represented and initiated by Gerald Travis Parnell, about as concise a portrait of a crooked city official as you'd hope to turn up. Florid and going a bit stocky (which is how "running to fat" often gets self-described in Texas) in his fifties, he leaned on the spoked arms of his antique command chair, creaking its springs as he spoke into the bulky old cellular phone held to his ear by one padded shoulder of an expensive double-breasted suit tailored from scratch ten years ago in Fort Worth, and showing the strain of containing his increasing "stock".

Perched with one scrawny buttock on the corner of his desk, Conrad Mallory, his lean Lincolnesque look a good clue to his legal profession but no sort of giveaway of his character, eavesdropped on the phone call. When Parnell punched the phone off and turned a wolfish grin to his partner in malfeasance, he returned a saturnine smile. "It's ironic, Jerry."

Having heard that one a time or two before, Parnell raised a bushy eyebrow. "Anything in particular?"

"Nope, everything about him." Mallory chuckled. "Hunstetter."

"I'll tell the world. Imagine Mister Limpo married to a hot dish like SueAnn. Hell, Mister BackEast working for a burg like this is strange enough."

"Then we come to the guy who actually floated the Stadium Bond in the first place being the only one who won't get any of it as a take-home prize."

"I still think we should cut him in a little," Parnell tossed out with the air of a man who's giving it his last try. "Just to be on the safe side."

"It doesn't work that way with those straight arrows. Offer him any sort of taste and he'd blow the whistle so loud they'd hear it in Austin."

"Too straight and just too damned lame. Anyway, she says he's not there. Went to the bank or something." He leaned sideways to stick the old cell phone in a belt holster hand-worked with the inimitable Texas flourishes, then pulled a sheaf of print-out from a drawer.

"What you got there?"

Parnell gave another predator grin. "Just some ball park figures."

Mallory chuckled and stood up, walked to the window to stare out the window at the parched square of "park" around the sand-blasted brick of the old courthouse. Yep. Ironic.

The greater size and less dilapidated standing of Sulfur Wells was apparent in the contrast between the lobby of its Miners Bank and the musty interior of the recently looted Chisolm establishment. Here

11

all was glass, blonde wood and commercial carpet, a showpiece with open teller stations to advertise modernity and trust. Equally blonde and open was Taffy, a pert teller very exemplary of the neighbor-girl beauty of the region, as typified by Cybill Shepherd and a procession of Miss America finalists. She bestowed a lovely smile on Alvin Hunstetter as she handed him one of those awkward-sized commercial bearer checks. Hunstetter, a CPA nerd so stereotypical that he had been mistaken for Eugene Levi on occasion, fumbled nervously as he slipped the shockingly large-denominated check into an inside pocket in his frumpy black suit.

"There you go, Mister Hunstetter," Taffy chirped vivaciously from the lush setting of her luxuriant palomino hair and fascinating cleavage. "Lot of trouble just to walk it up the street, huh?"

Hunstetter seemed pre-occupied, but wrenched his attention back to her. "Well, with my luck, I probably shouldn't try carrying this much cash."

Taffy's eyes widened and she jiggled in laughter. "Six million dollars? Lord, I guess not. We couldn't cash it anyway."

"That had occurred to me."

The baby blues narrowed in confusion. "You what?"

"Nothing, nothing. Thanks, Taffy." He turned to go but froze in his tracks as she chirped again.

"No problem, Mister Hunstetter. I already posted the transaction to the city by email, so you're set."

Horrified, he spun to face her. "You *what?* I mean... no need to do that. I haven't deposited it yet."

"Already updated," she beamed. "Isn't all this new technology amazing?"

12

Hunstetter backed away from her, his hand clutched to either the check or his heart. "Incredible," he stammered. "Dumbfounding."

Hunstetter emerged from the tinted glass doors of the bank dithering and distraught, jigging like a little boy who desperately needs a bathroom. At the sound of an airplane overhead, he jerked his arm up to consult his watch, then bolted across the sun-blasted parking lot, fumbled open his battered Pacer, and jumped in so quickly that he bounced up in pain from the hot plastic seat covers.

Once settled in, he reached into the pocket of his white button-down shirt and pulled out a comb. Pulling it through his sideburns--a half-inch long under his brisk flat-top--he seemed to relax a little. Pocketing the comb, he started the car and pulled out to the street in an obvious hurry.

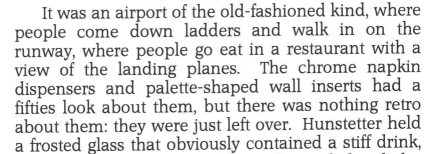

It was an airport of the old-fashioned kind, where people come down ladders and walk in on the runway, where people go eat in a restaurant with a view of the landing planes. The chrome napkin dispensers and palette-shaped wall inserts had a fifties look about them, but there was nothing retro about them: they were just left over. Hunstetter held a frosted glass that obviously contained a stiff drink, which was just as obviously greatly needed as balm to his nerves. Across from him a "Goodfella" type sipped coffee from a squat cup with ornate handle and aqua logo of stylized wings. His elbow rested on a medium-sized black briefcase.

"Nice public place," he said in the tone of somebody obviously trying to make idle small talk. "Plenty of witnesses."

That remark did absolutely nothing to unsaddle Hunstetter's nerves. Icecubes clinked in his glass as he gulped, "Witnesses?"

"Yeah, you know," the sharpie said casually. "In case we decide to keep the check and the money?"

Hunstetter jumped, then slumped, his eyes jittering in alarm, his body language pleading. "Oh, my God. You..."

"Relax." The guy in the Armani knockoff with bright blue shirt and black tie enjoyed the effect, but patted the air consolingly. "Just kidding. We don't want anything messy associated with this check. The whole idea is a nice, clean municipal draft. We run it around our laundry, it'll be pure as trackless snow. Cash is the problem nowadays. Your problem now." He pushed the briefcase toward Alvin with an understated flourish.

He touched the briefcase tentatively, with a touch of reverence. "Yes, I guess it is. This is it, then? I had assumed it would be larger."

The Goodfella leaned back, comfortable with the chance to show off. "Six thousand G-notes. You can get thousands easy in Vegas. Like silver dollars. Well, we can. You want small unmarked, bring a semi." He gestured at the briefcase like a conjurer. "Two hundred twenty three to an inch. Two fourteen inch rows, six inches wide. Just over thirteen pounds. Six kilos, even. Don't you think it's kind of poetic that a bill weighs a gram? It's like a *sign* to go buy drugs with it."

Hunstetter nodded, nonplussed.

The mobster made self-deprecating brush-off moves with his elegant hands. "Sorry, money fascinates me."

Staring at the briefcase, Hunstetter blurted, "Oh, me too."

14

That drew a burst of raucous laughter and a slap on the Formica tabletop. "I guess so. Know how many people it took to pile up this six million? And you did your end solo, right? Gotta hand it to you."

"It seemed like the only way to go," Hunstetter murmured, still under the spell of the briefcase.

"Well if you ever need a job..." the Fella began perfunctorily, then snapped his fingers. "Wait, on second thought..."

It took a second but Hunstetter nervously joined in the raucous laughter that gag provoked.

"Wish you'da took it in chips. Maybe we'd get some back." He picked up the already opened envelope and slipped in into his suit coat, then nodded. "Well, back to the salt mine. You heading for the gates? I'd guess you're leaving pretty soon, too."

Hunstetter stared longingly out the window at a jet taking off, but shook his head. "No.. Uh... something came up at the office. I need that lead. And can't let them trace any tickets... Ah, Jesus..."

"I sympathize." The gangster nodded sincerely. "Call me up. I'll comp you a room at the Baccarat."

He stood, shook hands warmly, then walked away, every step moving him further from any memory of Alvin Hunstetter. Who jumped up, threw down a bill, and headed for the exit holding the case to his chest with both arms.

CHAPTER THREE

A black scorpion dangled in mid-air, suspended only by two fine threads under its wicked looking pinchers and totally evil curved black tail. A totem of menace, even dread, it lowered slowly, swinging slightly.

"Careful, man!" Bogart snapped. "Don't let him fall."

"Pretty sure it's a him, huh, dickwad?" Flathead replied, annoyed at this kibitzing from his feckless partner.

"Careful, that's all."

"World to Bogart," Flathead said as the scorpion came into contact with a mold filled with clear, viscous fluid. "I'm not the one who fucks up everything he touches."

"Okay, okay," Bogart bubbled. "Now's when you can't make a false move, Bro." He leaned forward, totally concerned with the nasty arachnid being sunk in the gel.

"Asshole, who has been doing this all this time?" The scorpion broke the surface tension of the medium and slowly lowered towards the bottom of the mold.

"I'm just saying." As the scorpion came to rest on the bottom of the miniature mausoleum of acrylic resin, he breathed dramatically. "Way to go. Good, good. Now pull the threads out real slow, don't make any bubbles."

"That's what I'm gonna do. And soon as I do, I'm gonna strum your head with a torque wrench."

16

"Just be really cool," Bogart continued to coach. "Good, good... ah shit, a bubble." Sure enough, one thread left a tiny bubble, motionless in the clear gel, as it emerged.

"No big, fuckhole," Flathead snarled. "Watch this."

Bogie tipped back his grizzled, shaggy head to watch his partner, both of them seated at a redwood picnic table surrounded by the detritus of a biker camp: a moldy tent, two chopped Harleys, piles of mechanical parts, and middens of garbage. In turn surrounded by miles of what looked like "Stinking Desert National Monument".

Flathead, a tall, rangy biker in grungy leathers with wire spectacles and hair cut long to his shoulders but rigidly flat across the top, whipped out a big, serrated "Harley Davidson" brand sheath knife. He gripped it somewhat truculently while glaring balefully at his portly partner, whose rancid jeans, grimy hands and forearms, and head scarf printed with skeletons in sex positions provided a rustic setting for a sunburned face informed by the unquenchable childish delight of the truly stupid. Almost reluctantly, he bent over to slide the blade of the knife carefully into the mold, catch the bubble on its flat side, and gently nudge it to the surface, where it disappeared. The mold was now flawless, encasing the scorpion in a permanent plastic aspic. Around the mold were a stack of hardened Lucite bricks, each containing another belligerent scorpion or horrendous spider. The rest of the table was taken up with sun-bleached rattlesnake rattles and skulls yawning open to present their fangs. Bogart, holding a Lucite-encased tarantula and sheet of buffing paper, beamed at the latest casting. "A beauty, Flatty. Best one yet."

"Well, I had all that expert fucking advice."

17

"Hey, no problem, Bro," Bogart beamed. "Oughta bring ten bucks at the swap meet."

Flathead shrugged, sighed. "Boges, this isn't a particularly efficient way to make a living."

"That's how it is in the arts, man," the chubby bike bum shrugged. "But, hey, I've been telling you we could make some long green. You just don't have the balls."

"Oh, you've got enough for both of us." Flathead stood and leaned back to stretch, staring out across the blank, wavy air of the desert. "But it's not about balls; it's about ass. I just don't have enough ass to sit out another six years in the joint."

Bogart stopped buffing the gleaming prison of the tarantula belt buckle. "Was it worse than this?"

"You gotta point. Better food."

"Fine, you cook, then." But Bogart switched to a wheeling tone, "Look just a couple more runs. Use some of my ideas this time. Foolproof."

Flathead stiffen, his face working in rage. He leaned into Bogart, jabbing a finger into his face. "Don't you *ever*, man!"

His outrage at his partner, and the whole concept of foolproof, would require some background. So here it is, in immediacy-dripping present tense:

On a deserted airstrip, little more than a stomped-down soccer field for the itinerant cholla harvesters, really, a Piper Cub lowers from the sky, rocking slightly in the thermal upswell from the parched field. Wheeling at the end of the end of the cleared ground, it taxis up to what might have been called the terminal, had it not so generally been called a dilapidated piece of crap trying to finish falling down. The identification numbers of the plane are taped over, it's painted black. Two

18

windows sport little stars bestowed not by travel magazines, but by small-caliber gunfire. It's obviously up to no good.

Not a deterrent to Flathead and Bogie, by any means. They've been literally lying in wait, and when the plane halts outside the crumbling adobe shack and rusty gasoline truck, they jump up from under their dusty tarps and grab the solo pilot as he opens the door. Dragging him from the plane, they conk him a good one and tape him up.

Our heroes dump the fuming pilot in the shade of the hovel and start totin' them bales. Energized by mysterious forces, or perhaps substances, they make quick work of tossing several hundred pounds of tight-packed, burlap-wrapped, skunk-smelling, bulks of goldish/green vegetable substance into the little plane. Once their lading is complete, the two shaggy stevedores push the dragtail of the plane around and hop in. Bogie, shockingly, takes the pilot's seat and starts the engine. He pauses, revving, while Flathead--not generally the pious type--crosses himself and clenches his eyes shut. Grumbling slightly under its load of herbs and spices, the Piper rolls down the rutted runway. Twenty yards from the shed, a pair of shears ejects from the passenger side and the pilot starts the dirty, tiring business of humping towards them like a worm trying to shed its cocoon of duct tape. The take off is sloppy, but it happens and the perky piper heads back for the skies. It has sixty feet of sky under it as it passes over the thorny desert brush, and a stubby submachine gun with integral silencer flies out the passenger window, spinning down into the rough.

In the cockpit, Bogie takes an exaggerated vacuum cleaner suck from a giant spliff, whooping in childish glee as he pumps the flaps and jockeys the stick around with masturbatory gusto. Flathead, understandably, quails at this behavior, hanging on to dashboard in desperation. When Bogart does an exceptionally thrilling/idiotic swoop he screams and punches at his head, but the results *really* scare the shit out of him, so he subsides into a silent inner space of sheer terror.

Only partially explaining the attitude that would cause him to stab his finger more aggressively into Bogart's startled face, screaming, "...*EVER...*"

But perhaps another stirring flashback can shed some light on that:

Now five hundred shaky feet in the air and obviously no longer over Mexico, Flathead-- obviously wracked with the twin tribulations of trepidation and motion sickness--tosses bales out of the plane's open door. Easy to do because the Cub is listed over at almost thirty degrees as Bogie circles a stretch of cattle ranch chosen as their drop zone. When the last payload tumbles out, Flatty attempts to close the door, but it detaches from the plane and falls into empty space, planning like a kite as it heads for an unhappy ending below. He turns pleading eyes to Bogart, who nonchalantly hands him a parachute. Flathead freaks out completely, almost falling out the door in his efforts to avoid having to go out of it with the comfort of a canopy.

Harnessed into the 'chute, Flathead stands with one foot out on the landing gear strut and one in the plane scrambling for purchase to avoid falling off. He stares down into a personal hell, frozen. Bogart jerks the stick, dramatically yawing the plane, and his buddy tumbles out into space. He falls face up, screaming and flipping Bogie both fingers, until he hits the end of his improvised static cord and jerks like a hooked marlin before swinging in under his blossoming nylon umbrella.

Infinitely more cavalier about the perils of altitude, Bogie starts to jump from his door, then pauses and scrambles up on top of the plane, his weight shift causing it to dish around alarmingly. He stands on top, "surfing" and profiling like a chubby, ugly hood ornament, then does a stylized swan dive out into the blue yonder.

Spread-eagled like Rocky the flying squirrel, he soars ala Superman, zooming past Flathead, rocking to and fro under his 'chute. Flathead kicks at him as he plummets by, spits at him ineffectively.

The plane, deviated by Bogart's high dive theatrics, straightens up, but veers toward a distant populated area.

We're getting there. "There" being far to the east where, nominally safe in a tall office building in downtown San Antonio, various office drones move around their cubicles totally unaware of the existence of the two bike trash buddies. An ignorance soon to give way

21

to more pressing concerns. The first desk jockey to glance out the huge, bronze glass window of the secretary pool, probably dreaming of suntanning by the pool at her apartment, does a double-take, then jumps up horrified and screaming. She's joined in a general stampede away from the windows by the entire staff. But elevators are slow to respond to panic, and they stand with their backs pressed to the doors and wall, watching a black airplane without benefit of pilot approach the building at fifty pokey miles per hour.

The Piper enters the office prop first, due to its general configuration. This creates spectacular results. The spinning propeller chops the window into fragments instantly, and distributes them around the interior space with a democratic randomness. The whirlwind occasioned by having what is essentially an enormous, two-hundred horsepower fan suddenly enter the venue whirls the paper busywork into a swirling blizzard. Merely a prelude for the entrance of the main event, the fuselage itself. The stubby, graceless Cub body plows greedily into the office space, nudging desks and chairs into clumsy, but disastrous, flight of their own. Shedding both wings, which plunge to the street breaking several windows on their way down and creating untold consternation when they arrive in street traffic, the little Piper seems far from little as it shoulders it way into the floor, prop blades slashing objects like desk drawers, rolodex carousels, family portraits, calculators, and radios into line drives through walls into other

22

firms, through dropped ceilings, definitely including passage through windows and dividers.

Not, one gathers, the usual Friday afternoon at Southwest Fidelity Life.

"And I mean motherfucking *EVER, EVER...*" Flathead screamed (and by now the reasons for his reaction should be fairly clear) and punctuated his remarks by jamming his righteous finger right up Bogie's right nostril.

Moving forward with our backstory, if that makes sense, a major crowd attends Bogart and Flathead's arraignment. Bailiffs hustle them past the usual cameras and microphones, look a little worried at the ugly tenor of the mob behind the press. Flathead obviously shares their nervousness, covering his face with court documents while Bogart smiles at the cameras and hits poses in his bright red jail coveralls. The lack of sympathy for dope dealers who terrorize offices is evident and the call for long-term justice is strident. On the scene reporters hold microphones as they assure viewers that these clowns are going down. And, boy, have they got that right.

"...say 'foolproof' ever again!" Flathead thundered.
Bogart recoiled from the probings of his admonishing finger, deeply hurt. "What's on your ass, Bro? Going all freakin' booger bandido on me!"

CHAPTER FOUR

The leafy *palapa* provided shade for the flagstone patio and string hammock, but didn't block the view of the beach through the trunks of the coconut palms. An ocean breeze stirred the towels and swimsuits hanging on their line, just enough to keep things warm and balmy, instead of hot. The remains of shrimp *ceviche* tacos on the cement table had attracted the attention of the house iguana, who was ready to challenge two gulls for them. The radio played softly, a romantic trio laced with a filigree of guitars, almost covering the sound of the surf. Cole Haskins, wearing only a pair of floppy print swim trunks and a half-dozen clean white bandages, dozed in the hammock.

Bunny, wearing only snug pink panties, bent over a bucket, scrubbing in the suds. After a quick rinse in a big fluted Zapotec bowl, she reached up to hang her wash on the line. She'd already pinned up a few dozen freshly laundered greenbacks, and was having to stretch for room to find drying space for the latest bunch of moist fifties. Cole's eyes half-opened and he watched her from under his lashes: a fetching sight, indeed. She sensed his fond gaze and turned to face him, which opened his eyes the rest of the way.

"Now see, Buns?" he drawled, "And you keep claiming you got no domestic skills."

"Oh, now that's so funny. With us down to living on blood money."

Cole stretched, then idly scratched his washboard stomach. "Not the blood, so much. It's that damned explosion paint."

24

She felt around the bowl, then the bucket, and inspected the row of bills flapping softly in the breeze. "I figure we got about six more months."

"If you'da held off a few more seconds for your demo derby back there, I'da scooped up another year or so."

Bunny sighed, grabbed her Corona in its faded "Cabo Wabo" foam sleeve and came over to squat by the hammock. "I'm starting to question your bright idea of coming to a place where we don't speak the language and aren't allowed to get jobs."

"Jobs?" Cole stared at her in overblown horror. "Why, I'd no more let a wife of mine take a job than I'd get one myself. This place is perfect."

"It's beautiful, lover. But if you'd take a little practical notice..."

"What I practically notice is a few things like armored cars down here are easy, security systems suck, and the cops are a bad old joke."

Bunny sipped her beer and rolled her eyes. "Oh, sure thing, Sundance. Let's learn Spanish so we can do holdups for money that's barely worth the paper it's printed on."

"Hey, you can trade it for real money. Just like we trade those bills there for pesos to buy chow."

"There's extradition here, Cole. If our names so much as show up on a winning lottery ticket we'll be on a plane in handcuffs."

"You figure that'd be worse than jail down here?"

"I seriously doubt it. But it'd be no picnic with robbery and accessory charges, vehicle mayhem."

"Don't forget Driving On Sidewalks."

She finished her beer and set it down with a definitive gesture. "So just forget it, Sugar. We'll have to figure on something else."

Cole reached out to lightly stroke the side of her breast with the backs of his fingers. "Well, I could put you out on the street corner, I guess. Doing what you do bettern anybody I ever..."

Oops. That one drove Bunny into a sudden rage. She popped to her feet, grabbing the hammock and jerking it around, jostling him.

"Cole, you little *jerk!* What I do best is pick up after a man spoiled too rotten to support a family."

Cole suffered the hammock spins with a doting smile, but when Bunny socked him a couple of times, he winced. She instantly switched to her lovebird mode, hovering over him. "Oh, no, honeybunch, did I mess up your wounds?"

"Not so's I'd notice. But I ain't a hundred percent yet, Lambkins."

She fluttered and nurtured, checking his dressings and smoothing down his hair. "Couldn't prove it by me, Sweet Pea. Even with a few chunks missing, you're more man than I ever need."

"Sometimes times of need ain't all that bad."

She slipped out of the panties and carefully slid onto the hammock beside him, spooning in behind him to cuddle and pet. The hammock stopped swinging after a while, but gradually took up other rhythmic forms of motion.

CHAPTER FIVE

Driving with the briefcase snugged up against his right thigh, Alvin Hunstetter approached a severe new parking structure across the street from City Hall. He headed into the ramp, but suddenly froze-- his Pacer sitting motionless in the street as if reading the PARKING FOR CITY EMPLOYEES ONLY sign. He stared at the building as horns blared behind him and drivers he'd blocked gunned past him yelling insults he didn't hear. He reached a decision and cut his wheel left, accelerating away from the parking area he had suddenly seen as a trap.

Finding a vacant space on a side street with little traffic, Alvin parked and carefully checked through the car. He climbed out and started up the street, briefcase clenched tightly in his hand. Again he froze up, dithering on the sidewalk. After a long, motionless cogitation, he headed back to the car and opened the trunk. After looking around very carefully to see if he was observed, he stashed the briefcase inside, dumping an old blanket and a bag of golf clubs on top of it. Locking up carefully, he peered around again, then stood back to beep the alarm. He pulled out his comb and glided it through his sideburns for a long moment, then hurried off, glancing back at the car several times before reaching the corner and turning towards City Hall.

The city's embezzling accountant stood outside the lobby doors, for a long, pregnant moment, staring inside. Then he took a deep breath, pushed the glass doors open, and strolled in like he owned the place. Or at least he thought so: many would have seen his walk through the lobby as a guilty slouch. Heading for the elevators, he made it a point to give a jaunty nod to the desk cop on duty. In the elevator he turned and pushed the button for the fifth floor. As the doors shuddered shut he saw the cop at the desk staring right at him, speaking rapidly into the receiver of a telephone while grabbing for a microphone on coiled cord. The doors closed completely and he desperately stabbed the third floor button.

When the doors opened on Three, Hunstetter exited the car in a jitterbug panic. He ran up the hall one way, then reversed and tore off the other way. He pounded his head for ideas, then fell to his knees for a moment of prayer. But before the Lord could respond with advice on getting away with stealing millions of dollars he'd been trusted with, the elevator gave a crisp, ominous ding and he jumped up and dashed to a stairwell door. Nipping inside, he held it open a crack, peering out at developments in the hallway he'd just vacated in fear.

The elevator opened and he was dismayed to see Captain Garvey step out. He knew the most respected cop on the force, of course. First name basis, had lunch with him a few times. But at the moment it was all about CAPTAIN GARVEY being there, and for the obvious, expressed purpose of tracking him down. One look at Garvey's tall, outdoorsy figure and rumpled uniform and he was aware as never before that he was now very solidly on The Wrong Side Of The Law.

Garvey moved with a casual, confident economy, casing the hallway as two young cops Hunstetter knew by sight, but not by name, moved to flank him. One freckled, the other very callow-looking, two young jocks in their twenties dying to impress their hero and role model. The Captain motioned to left and right and the young cops moved down the hall, trying doors.

"Remember," Garvey cautioned in his soft Gulf Coast drawl, "He knows this building upside down. He's got keys. Don't skip any closets, shitters, nothing."

A radio crackled and the freckly cop whipped it from his belt and listened as Garvey peered through a doorway and checked behind the door before pulling it closed.

"It's Heinz, Captain," he heard the callow cop say in a taut "official" voice. "Nobody got off on Five."

"Maybe," Garvey said, still looking around the empty hallway with lazy eyes. "Check it all real careful, boys."

Appalled, Hunstetter eased the door closed and fled down the stairs.

Busting from the stairwell, Hunstetter shot desperate glances around, running futile patterns of confusion and flight reflex. He pulled out a slim cellular phone and started punching in a number. Coming to a sudden realization, he reacted violently, slamming the phone shut with a shudder. He stared wide-eyed at the phone for a second, then tossed it into a waste receptacle.

The decisive, final movement seemed to steady him, because he drew himself up, visibly tugging himself together. He pulled out the comb and raked his sideburns a few slow passes. Settled down considerably, he approached an empty office, glanced around, and pulled out a keychain to open the door.

Sitting under a desk, Hunstetter cradled a phone receiver to his ear to muffle it. He hunched

29

protectively, listening furtively for the opening of the door. He spoke quietly, even though he was obviously deeply annoyed. "Harlan, if you'll just tear yourself away from your addiction for five seconds, here, I've got a real creampuff for you. It'll rack up some major storage charges because the guy's going to jail for six months, minimum."

He listened, scowling, holding the phone with both hands as he beat it against his forehead. Under his breath he hissed, "Moron!"

Into the phone he spoke with elaborate calm. "Could you *please* just pause that game a second? Ah. Don't thank me now." Some sound outside the office caught his ear and he glanced around nervously, then spoke in total exasperation. But quietly. "How would I know how SueAnn is? She moved out, remember? With the kids and everything else of value."

Again he listened as though holding back from biting a piece out of the phone. "*You* ask her, Harlan. She's your sister. Got a pencil? Paper? You have to move really fast on this impound or they'll give it to Archibald's. Ready?"

Hunstetter squatted on the rim of a toilet bowl in a narrow stall of new, but abused walls. He could hear measured steps approaching, sounding to him like shots echoing on the white tile floors. The feet stopped, a stall door creaked open, they came closer. Toes of highly polished black work boots appeared beneath the stall door, facing him. He sighed, pulled himself together with great effort, stepped down off the stool, and flushed it. Brushing himself off, he suddenly shook with a tremor like a wet dog, then

30

opened the door to see Captain Carl Garvey standing there looking at him, a little sadly.

"Hey, Al," the Captain said, "Got a minute?"

"Actually. I'm a little rushed." What he actually was, he was at the point of losing it completely. He reached inside his coat for the solace of his comb. A slight alteration of posture and attitude showed Garvey to be very much open for business.

"Let's keep 'em out where we can admire that manicure, okay, Al?" he said, and Hunstetter's heart sunk. Served notice that the proverbial jig was completely up, he slowly pulled the comb out and compulsively slid it through his sideburns.

"Let's go chat a spell." Garvey said, companionably.

Numb, Hunstetter turned and tottered toward the door with Garvey a pace behind him.

"Hey, Al?"

"Hunstetter's shoulders clenched and he turned with a pleading face.

Garvey shrugged towards the basins. "Aren't you gonna wash your hands?"

CHAPTER SIX

Bogart just beamed. Radiating pride, he poured questionable Mexican gasoline from a rusty surplus jerry can into his grimy chopper. The bike itself was such an amalgam of parts from his previous scoots, cannibalized wrecks, and earstwhile owners that Bogie thought of as "donors", and general jury-rigging and swapping out that it had become generic: a vehicle without model year, VIN number, specific engine size, or any general category other than "100% Harley". He poured carefully, though, so as not to get more gas on the already pitted and discolored paint job on his tank: a fading picture of a reclining woman so naked and buxom as to make any position other than reclining fairly unfeasible. And apparently fornicating or miscegenating or whatever with a huge red scorpion. But it wasn't even that trophy he was so proud of. He was once again an innovator, an unsung genius of the deceptively simple activity of transporting goods from one side of an imaginary line to the other side. A vocation not, as we've seen from the flashbacks, without its ups and downs.

"It's just so perfect," he gloated. "Who's going to think of there being anything in the gas tank?

"Anybody who saw 'Easy Rider'," Flathead replied, but without denting his partner's buoyant spirits.

The Boge tossed the can out into the desert, snapped the cap, and slapped the tank affectionately. "We make a run to The World, pull the tank, fish it out, and... *voyla.*"

"Should work," Flatty admitted reluctantly. "How much tubing did it take?"

32

Bogie turned intense attention to polishing the tank's scarred surface. "Well, thing is, we didn't have any big tubing."

Flathead said merely, "So...." but there was a rising inflection of tension in his voice.

"So I just double-bagged it, duct-taped it good. Don't worry, it's tighter than whale pussy."

The hint of stress in Flathead's tone rose to warning levels. "Baggies? You used *baggies?*"

"Sure man. What we always use." *Now* what was the hassle?

"They dissolve in gasoline, you stupid, stupid, STUPID motherfucker!"

He jumped Bogart, pounding on him with both fists and both boots, but the chubby biker was more agile than he looked and avoided major damage. If he could just explain... "Wait, *wait!* It's in caps anyway."

Flathead groped around for a rock, found only an empty oil can, which he fired at the fat pink face. "Oh, the gelatin capsules that dissolve in your stomach? You fuck up everything, you moron scuzz."

Abashed and faced with the probable ruin of his inventive genius, Bogie stroked the tank ruefully. "This has to be the highest test gasoline in Mex, Tex, or Okie."

"At a thousand bucks a gallon, it fucking well should be." Flatty had found an old army entrenching tool and was swinging at his partner, who ducked, but had another brainstorm.

"Hey, think it'd improve performance? I mean, why do you think they call it speed?"

Spurred to action by the radical implications of that concept, he sidestepped another charge, pounced on the chop and kicked it into a thunderous roar.

Flathead stopped in spite of himself, curious, as the grease bucket revved up and spun out in a cloud of alkali dust. Bogie whooped and hollered for thirty yards before the bike coughed, hacked, and died.

Flathead stood, staring at him, then lowered his head on his chest, shaking it in an autistic motion. "Brokedick retardo son of a bitch."

CHAPTER SEVEN

A warehouse full of strangers with forty watt bulbs. Exposed toilets and stainless steel sinks with no hot water tap. Concrete and iron painted over so often it looked like cast rubber. Floor or rigid bench: take your pick.

For some reason Hunstetter still had a seat on the bench, possibly because his attempts to defensively hunch himself into total invisibility was partially working. But not for long.

When the clump of raw-boned, predatory cons from the court chain got tired of not impressing each other with chilling tales of bravado and badassery (chilling, certainly, to Hunstetter) they got around to noticing the soft, timid fawn in the middle of their wolfpack and paid him some attention. He could have done without it.

A stringy-haired white boy who anybody else in the holding tank could have made as a junkie (and total punkass) in a hot second walked over in his lace-less boots, trying to achieve the effect of being bigger than five and a half feet by striding ponderously and making hand gestures that looked like he copied them from old bronze statues in courthouse yards. He stood in front of Hunstetter, rocking back and forth in his old jump boots, until he caught his extremely reluctant eye. He opened the conversation with, "Spare a square, bitch."

Hunstetter jerked as if slapped, and shot his eyes around the circle of coveralled yardbirds, receiving cold comfort, if any at all. "What?" He stammered. "A square? I don't..."

A tough looking Chicano in one of those mohawk mullets even the *cholos* stopped wearing five years before pushed up beside the cracker, hands thrust down into the crotch of his carefully ripped jumpsuit, his (totally fake) tattooed teardrops framing cold Rio Grande-jumping eyes, and sneered, "*Frajo, ese.* Fockin' cigarette."

Hunstetter had never smoked so much as one puff of anything, ever, in his life, but patted his pocketless chest, murmuring, "Sorry, I don't have..."

There was raucous laughter of bad omen, and he felt his anus clench in a useless protective reaction. But there were more offerings on the smorgasbord of multi-racial menace. A black inmate who Hunstetter thought of as enormous, as well as totally terrifying, loomed up behind his colleagues, glowering down from a scarred, scowling face presented between a shaven skull and brontosaurus pectorals. Catching, or more like mugging, the horrified CPA's eye, he smiled an egregious smile and licked yards of limber lips. Hunstetter's anxious sphincter almost unclenched over that one, and he barely held his water as this out-of-Africa behemoth simpered, "What got your sweet pale ass in here, woman? Little *white* collar crime?"

The jailbirds cackled like manic magpies and the circle started to constrict on the hapless Hunstetter. Always forthcoming, however, he almost whispered, "I stole... I 'ripped off' the city."

The toughs loved it. "*Hijole!*" the Chicano carjacker brayed. "You some sort of Robin Hood *vato*? Gonna kick us down?"

"Damn, oughta give you a medal," the huge black mugger chuckled. "How much you take 'em down for?"

"Uh..." Hunstetter cleared his throat. "Six million dollars. Rounded up."

The silence resonated out of the cell so dramatically that one of the deputies looked up from his magazine to see if anything atrocious was going on. Finally the redneck junkie coughed and said, "Hooooly shit. Hey, wanna smoke?"

CHAPTER EIGHT

Cole didn't need to look to assemble the parts of the big revolver, lying cleaned and oiled on the *huanacaxle* wood table in the pleasantly pulsing gold glow of a propane lantern. He put them together with sure, spare movements while looking at something far better; Bunny in sexy peasant/houri nightwear leaning in to examine her flawless features in the wall mirror. She regarded herself pensively and pitilessly, then turned, posing just so.

"Look at me Cole."

Like she had to ask. He was obviously liking what he saw.

"Do I look like Ma Barker to you?" Obviously an academic question, but the kind men answer at their peril. "Would I make some good old gun moll?"

She ignored him shaking his head, and gave her walk over to the table a lot of extra oomph, "I'm young and beautiful, Honey. I want to live it out, don't you see? Glamour, romance, exotic settings. With a beautiful man."

Compressing the cylinder spring by feel while slipping the cam down and turning it fast, Cole stayed fixed on her face and said, "You used to think running with me was glamorous and romantic enough."

"Well, yeah, compared to living in that old truck stop out of Nacogdoches. But I've seen more now, and I want more. Is that so bad?"

"Bad?" He was incredulous at the very idea. "Anything you want is okay with me, Darlin'. You know that. We'll figure out how to move you into one of those magazine covers that give you all these ritzy ideas, okay?"

38

"Aw, Sweetie. You always know how to soften me up." And she was looking softer and more accommodating by the minute, her loose top sagging and flowing with lush visions.

"It's a chore, but somebody's gotta. How about you set your hard ass over here on my lap now? I got my own theories about romance."

CHAPTER NINE

The bronze wedge on the cluttered old dry goods desk displayed the legend, "MAURICE BATTLES: BAILOUT MF". And nothing about Battles cast any doubt on the title. He'd be over fifty, with the look of a failed middleweight who wouldn't fail to come out of a bar brawl standing and taking names. The cramped office shack had few personal touches; an autographed picture of Kareem Abdul Jabar, a clock mounted in brass baby shoes, a rack of shotguns and aluminum softball bats. Although the latter were possibly more in the category of professional equipment. The Battles firm tended to draw its clientele from the lower and less stable ranks of the recently incarcerated.

He leaned back in an odd, Scandinavian-looking "Better Back Store" chair, feet holding down stacks of the mutating colonies of paperwork bred and nourished by what people, with no trace of irony, call the criminal "justice" "system". His eyes were warm and soft in a cold, hard face and his voice sounded like he could have played "De Lawd" in a black theater group's version of Green Acres. A property wasted on the venal dickhead on the other end of the telephone he held almost delicately to his ear.

As he spoke he had the full attention of Mallory, seated in front of his desk in a severely strait chair he had picked up to discourage a lot of hanging out. "Yeah, Mallory's right here," he informed the phone. "Was him told me to call. Because otherwise, I gotta tell you..."

He broke off to listen, his eyes suddenly cutting to Mallory, and not in a fond way. "Damn straight, it's too rich for my blood. But more like, it stinks."

40

He listened further, nothing he was hearing jollying up his expression. "Like bringing pressure on me. License, permits, access: you know the crap."

His gaze jolted again to Mallory, who smiled serenely. "Whoa, I guess you *do* know. But if you're down with it..."

He broke off to listen again, then laughed like an amused Rottweiler. "The *city*? Shit, Mallory damn near *is* the city. And I doubt the whole town's worth that much. They said you'd lay the whole thing off."

He relaxed a little, fiddling with some bullets and antacid tablets on his desk as he listened.

"All right, then. What I needed to know. Usual deal?"

The answer clouded his face over. "Shit, that's a pretty unusual price on the usual deal, but it don't sound like neither of us got much choice in this whole shitaree."

He scowled at Mallory while getting more sorry news, then said, "Yeah, yeah. Send it on. But the point is, you got my ass."

Hanging up, he leaned forward in his chair to glower at Mallory. "So I guess we got a deal. You wanna call it that."

With more of his limitless supply of serene regard, Mallory purred, "I'd call it civic pride."

"Shit. That's so lame I just gotta hear it."

"We need him out because he absconded with the stadium funds."

Battles nodded. "So they reportedly allege."

"You have to be far-sighted. That ballpark, the Twins doing spring training here, there's going to be a lot more money coming into town."

"A sweet deal for so many, I'd guess."

"Float a lot of boats."

"Got yours all picked out? Here's some ghetto wisdom for you: when there's cement gets poured, there's money gets whored."

"Pithy. Everybody's Johnny Fuggin Cochran these days."

Battles' eyes rolled up beseechingly. "Oh, pleeease.   That jiveass twerp?   I'm old school. Mohammed Fuggin' Ali."

"Thing is, it all trickles down. More white money means more 'Negro' thieves, more bail customers."

"Now, you know, that's why I find the company of white folk so expanding. I'd never have thought of it that way. But thing is, niggers bail on a grand, maybe two. Not six million."

"See? We're putting you into the big league seats already."

"I guess. I never wrote a treasurer before. I'm guessing they're not as bugass as your average mope."

"Alvin's solid. Unimaginative."

Battles laughed a good one over that.   "He allegedly imagined jaking your asses for you.

As unsure and tentative leaving the cell block as entering it, the disgraced treasurer stood at the caged window of a dreary booking office, holding his pants up with one hand, his belt and laces in the other. His rumpled street clothes were a good match for his three-day stubble and clueless expression. He had to juggle his belt to take the manila envelope of personal effects the bored clerk handed him, then put it all down to sign the clipboard where the clerk pointed. As he fumbled his stuff into his pockets another released con stepped to the window and Hunstetter had his arms full of useless junk and

42

paperwork as he turned to the grubby plastic chairs in the waiting area.

Where Maurice Battles, natty in a camel hair coat and reversed tan wool Kangol, stepped over to him, brandishing a sheaf of official-looking papers. "Got it right here, my man."

Hunstetter stared. "Got what?"

Battles proffered the papers and gave a deprecating gesture around the depressing waiting area. Grinning, he told him, "The key to this here Bastille."

CHAPTER TEN

The moon was a glorious host, afloat over gilded waters, the palms quivered sexily in the light breeze, the waves did not break; they lapped.

And in a hammock between two of those palms, Cole Haskins and Bunny Beaumont tussled; naked, torrid and tempestuous. At the moment, Bunny was doing most of the moaning, while Cole maintained a cool, persuasive ministration. "This is no time to talk about...." she gasped. "Aw, jeez, Cole."

"Now you going to turn me down, here, Sugar Booger?" Cole wheedled as she clawed at his buttocks and chewed on his shoulder. "Tell me not to?"

"No baby. We can't... Oh, God do that again. Come on, Sugar, what the hell you doing here?"

"So you're saying you'll at least think about it?"

"*Think?* Jesus Christ, boy! Ahhhhhh, sweet Christ almighty. Oh, yeah. Do that, honey. Do that."

"Did I hear a 'yes' in there?"

"*Fuck* you, dammit Cole. Ah, yes. Yes, yes, yes, yeesss."

A crescendo of inarticulate yelps ensued, followed by growls, yowls and gesticulations. Eventually leading down to cocoon twirls in the hammock, signs of release, sighs, and a long pause. At some point Bunny, very softly, said, "I just can't say no to you, can I?"

"Kinda why I took up with you in the first place, maybe you recall."

"You are such a humongous asshole."

The soothing sounds of tropic night wore on for a while, the hammock slowed down almost to a halt.

44

Then Bunny muttered, "Okay. My turn to be the asshole."

"You're better at it anyway," Cole said in a sleepy voice. Then, in a sharper tone, proclaimed, "Whoooah!"

CHAPTER ELEVEN

The sun-parched, God-forsaken flats were bisected by forty yards of cheap red wire, staked a foot and a half of the ground. Bogart and Flathead crouched beside the southernmost stake, looking very disappointed in a scruffy, but defiant, male coyote.

The coyote would gladly have parted company with these two lunatics that had trapped him, tricked him out and hauled him out here for whatever unwholesome experiment they were trying to run. He looked far from fashionable in the heavy collar, a studded bondage model Bogie had purchased in an "adult" store but given up on finding any humans to model for him. The collar had a ring on it for attaching leashes or whatever accessory adults might attach to such a thing. The wire was threaded through the ring so for the moment the coyote's options were limited to either running along the wire to the other stake, or hunkering down and trying to figure out how to gut these assholes and chew its way out of this mess. He had opted for the latter.

An incongruous contrast to the porno collar was the spiffy nylon pooch pack they'd strapped on him: bright red ballistic nylon, possibly even Gore-Tex; the perfect thing for the happy pets of yuppie outdoorspersons to wear on a campout, carrying their own share of the provisions. The coyote didn't appreciate that gift, either.

Bogart, sensing that the silence had lingered on and become somewhat recriminatory, looked at the upside, as usual. "It's a workable idea. We just got a totally unmotivated coyote here."

"That rabbit wasn't exactly a self-starter, either."

46

Bogart scowled at the memory of the sorry excuse for a jackrabbit. "Look, that fucker was haywire right from jump. I think we can work with this guy."

"Maybe we shoulda brought a roadrunner."

"I got better motivation than that," Bogie exclaimed, awash in yet another brainstorm. He popped the snappy FasTex closers on the PupPack, revealing a handful of white bindles inside. Pulling one of those creepy plastic twenty peso notes out of his wallet, he rolled it up and tamped if full of white powder from one of the baggies. Flathead, shaking his head in disbelief and scorn, watched him grab the struggling coyote's snout, insert the bill in one nostril, and blow into the other end. He released the now super-jazzed animal and stood, radiant with admiration of his latest plan.

The coyote shook his head and snorted a few times, then snapped at him and ran. It made it about six paces along the wire before coming to a halt, violently shaking.

"Attaboy! Go for it!" Bogart yelled, jumping with clenched fists like a cheerleader. "Dig! Dig, dig, dig!"

The little beast fell over, rigid legs kicking, every hair standing on end, and quaked in the icky *caliche* dust of the old lake bed.

"On your feet, sport!" Bogart bellowed. "Aw, man."

The bikers walked over to the animal, squatted to examine it. Flathead stood again, disgusted. "You fried the little fucker, Boge."

His partner hated to accept defeat, but could hardly deny it. He stood slowly, searching for a sunny side to the flopped smuggling scheme. "Ah, shit. Well, at least he died happy."

"Oh, no doubt," Flathead sneered, staring down at the animal's bulging, bloodshot eyes and tooth-baring grimace. "Check out that blessed-out look on his face."

Bogie sulked, kicking unhappily at the silt.

"Isn't this a little too complex?" Flatty asked him.

"What?" Bogart bleated. "It's just got a few bugs."

"Why don't we just get one of those shock collars they use to train hunting dogs? Left, right, stop, run like a motherfucker. We could steer him across the border like one of those radio controlled planes."

Bogart's face came up, painted with wild surmise. "Planes? Then why would need the damned coyotes and shit?"

Flathead stared at him, unable to believe, but starting to, anyway. "Bogie, sometimes you're not as stupid as you most times are."

CHAPTER TWELVE

Back at the unpreposing Sulfur Wells Municipal Airport, Hunstetter was an inch away from jumping right out of his pallid skin as he slunk up to the baggage check counter, schlepping what he didn't realize was a totally suspicious-looking K-Mart duffle bag up on the scale. Preoccupied with the whole business of tags and stubs and fiendishly concealed last-minute fees, he didn't notice a nearby loiterer, so bland of aspect and carefully generic of wardrobe that you'd just know he was some sort of surveillance operative. For the first time in his life, Alvin Hunstetter had a following.

Carefully tucking his claim stub into his boarding pass envelope, Hunstetter headed for the departure gates with his underseat-sized carry-on. The ostentatiously surreptitious tail watched the dufflebag disappear down a conveyor belt and through the rubber-flapped pet door. Among other things, he was wondering why the hell they'd installed this fancy new conveyor system when there was only one runway and bags just got tossed on a cart outside. This ain't DFW, he was thinking as he turned and stalked after Hunstetter. He continued his lurking, noticeable to everybody except the dweeb he was tailing, as the spooked accountant clumsily shoved his carry-on into the X-ray device, emptied his pockets into a paper bucket obviously intended for fried chicken, and stepped into the detector gate. Immediately the gate went on red alert and sounded several alarms, one audible on the spot.

The alarm sounding was not a novelty to the porky little security guardette with ragged mouse-colored bangs tickling her acne outbreaks. The local yokels had diddled the voltage array up to a sensitivity that would take a jaundiced view of a large tooth filling. But she lost her customary boredom at her first glance at the ghostly inner view of Hunstetter's carry-on. She hit the brakes on the advance, backed it up six inches, and stared with her mouth open wide enough to reveal the flavor of her chaw of gum. (Kiwi Fruit Chew: she'd gotten into airport work out of a taste for the exotic that had yet to be fulfilled.)

She goggled at the innocuous sight of Hunstetter, sitting on a table removing his shoes under the enforcing eye of a muscular male guard she'd had a brief crush on until she'd made the mistake of attending a tractor pull with him and watching him eat a chili dog. She was leaning on the little red button and frantically gesticulating at her supervisor while jabbing an accusing finger at Hunstetter. Her supe moved quickly towards the gate, motioning for her to calm down and not alert this fiendishly disguised terrorist into setting something off.

As the supervisor and a uniformed airport police officer arrived, both stimulated to dramatic alertness levels by what the fat chick's gnawed fingernail was pointing to on the scanner monitor, the big guard had narrowed the area of his concern down to Hunstetter's left shoe, which he treated to both electronic and visual inspection. Ignoring coughs and hisses from the scanner console, he pulled out the padded insole and inverted the shoe. The airport cop had his hand on his new Glock when a little disk--blatantly and unapologetically an electronic signaler, fell out into his ham-like hand. He picked it up between two fingers, turned to show it to the chubbo at the scanner, who he still wouldn't mind sharing some sweat with, and stared into the gaze of his boss and a cop pointing one of those silly-looking plastic Taser pistols.

Staring at this unsuspected footwear accessory, Hunstetter struggled to hide the dismay he was experiencing at realizing he was in way over his head. He held up the disk, noted the crisp circuitry and quasi-military intimation of purpose, and shuddered.

The big guard waved a dismissive meathook at it. "One of those anti-shoplifting gizmos. We find a few all the time. Just shitcan it." He nodded in the direction of a trashcan and handed Hunstetter his shoes, but there was no time to try them on before the Supervisor and cop arrived, looking stern but also a little thrilled that something was actually happening for once. Glancing at his carry-on, cradled cautiously in the arms of supervisor, Hunstetter blinked owlishly.

Taken aback by this development, his tail drifted closer, confirming his thoughts when he heard Hunstetter remonstrating, "Please, I *have* to catch that flight. It's extremely important."

In the bland vacuity favored by official interactions, the supe told him, "This shouldn't take long, sir."

"But my luggage is checked through to Miami. I'm not a terrorist or anything! I'm a CPA!"

"Nobody is accusing you, sir," the supe said in far from soothing tones. "Yet."

The tail watched, unable to decide what to make of it all, as Hunstetter was firmly escorted to a plain door off to one side.

Inside the stuffy, bare white security station, Hunstetter stood, radiating calm as the Supervisor stared at him with folded arms while the cop and guard rifled his bag.

Tensions mounted noticeably when the guard gingerly pulled a compact submachine gun out of the carry-on. The cop went full alert immediately as the supervisor tore his eyes off the gun to shoot a startled look at the mild-mannered city treasurer. Hunstetter broke out into shrill laughter and slapped himself on the forehead.

"I don't think it's a real gun, Sir," the guard announced, highly disappointed that everyone was safe.

"Make no assumptions," the cop growled.

"They call them 'airsoft'. They're plastic." He pointed at the wall and pulled the trigger. A small, bright orange ball shot out of the barrel and bounced off the wall, hitting the supervisor in the temple. He glared at the guard, but turned his attention back to Hunstetter.

"I am *so* sorry. I never thought of that. It's a present for my nephew. Look, I apologize..."

The supervisor was far from mollified, but nodded huffily. The guard grinned at the cop, who glowered at Hunstetter in frustration.

"No apology necessary, Sir," the supervisor said, the all-caps official tone now a bit oily. "I'm sure you understand our need for precaution."

"Oh, absolutely," Hunstetter assured him. "I fly a lot and appreciate you keeping us safe. This is just so embarrassing."

"Very understandable Mister..." he consulted the ticket quickly, "Hunstetter. Mister Hale will help you repack. I'm afraid I have to confiscate the... 'gun', though."

52

Hunstetter nodded understandingly, then suddenly went stiff, gasped and slumped into one of the tacky fiberglass chairs. Instantly the other men in the room were back in consternation mode. Had he taken poison? Was it a feint? Would an alien emerge from his guts?

"Oh, no," he said in a strained voice. "It must have been the excitement. It'll pass."

The supervisor didn't like the looks of it at all, and approached Hunstetter solicitously. "Are you all right, Sir? Do you require attention?"

"Heart condition," Hunstetter blurted. "Very slight. Not to worry." He grabbed a pill vial and water bottle from his carry-on, fumbled a pill into his mouth and sipped. Subsiding, he touched his chest.

"Can I do anything else for you, Mister Humsettler?" the supervisor asked, rather hoping for a negative answer.'

"I've been too much trouble already." Hunstetter gave him a weak smile. "But could I just sit here awhile? Catch my breath a little?"

In the main terminal, the secretive tail drew curious glances as he snarled into his cell phone in frustration. Was that guy some sort of Secret Servant, or something?

"I have no idea how he got on the plane, but that's where the tracer puts him. He's nowhere around and it leaves in five minutes. He checked the bag to Miami. Unless you can hold it here, you'd better have somebody meet it in Florida."

Still staring at the office door where Hunstetter had vanished, he listened with little visible enjoyment. "Okay, call him now. His name's Dawes? Where is he?"

His eyes flicked up to the office doors on the mezzanine where the SkyVue Lounge was located. "I see it. I'm there." He pocketed the phone and hustled for the stairs to the mezzanine.

As Hunstetter, clutching his carry-on, cautiously opened the door and peered around. Taking a deep breath, he hustled out the door and towards the terminal's parking lot entrance. The automatic glass doors whisked shut behind him, cutting off the loudspeaker announcement, "Southwest Airlines Flight 376 to Miami will experience a slight delay in departure. Will Southwest passenger Alvin Hunstetter please come to the red courtesy phone?"

He scrabbled across the lot, hugging his luggage and shooting his eyes around frantically in fear of seeing some dire new development. His plan was working, but the hidden sensor had spooked him considerably. As he walked around behind the canopied trailer with the sign "VALUE CAR RENTAL", he wondered idly what would have happened if he'd gotten on the plane with the bug in his shoe–instead of dropping it into that fat lady's purse at the scanner. Would they have considered it one of those "electronic devices" you were supposed to extinguish at take-off? The back of the rental office trailer had another sign, "SAVE ON LOW MILEAGE FLEET CARS", An employee, wearing a plaid polyester sportcoat over blue jeans and a red satin shirt, stepped out of the trailer and caught up to him beside the rather fatigued-looking Toyota Tercel with a chipped windshield banner proclaiming, "FACTORY AIR".

CHAPTER THIRTEEN

If Mallory's office in the executive building of "Sulfur Smells" was dowdy, Con Parnell's was positively Spartan. The bare walls were not off-white, but exactly on white. The old-fashioned glass-fronted oak shelf units held only thick cloth-covered legal books, his roll-top was not only spotless, but featureless, without a single object in sight. A plain black frame held his law degree from Hardin Simmons. He sat stiff and motionless with the receiver of his antiquated black phone to his ear, then hung it up without any comment.

Mallory leaned forward from another of the severe oaken chairs, hands on his knees. Both men stared into middle distance for a long moment, then Mallory spoke. "Well, now, then."

Parnell nodded grimly. "Just our luck. That limpdick beancounter finally gets clever just when he has our entire stadium fund. What Gods did we offend?"

"At times like this," Mallory said slowly, "I find luck to be over-rated."

"Well, I don't see much of a role for staunch work ethic in turning this one around."

"Also over-rated. What comes through in the real disasters is irony."

Parnell snorted disdainfully at that sentiment. "Who'd guess it to look at him?"

"Yep. Google 'nerd' and you'd get 187,543 pictures of Hunstetter."

"And now he's late-blooming into a one-man catastrophe. The city's out six million, maybe the whole spring training program. That bail bond clown is going to eat another six mill. He's our own personal Hurricane Katrina."

"Let's go have another talk with that jig bondsman."

"Think he'll have any irony for us?"

"Just could be," Mallory mused. "And I think I can just make it out from here."

"See what?"

"Let's just call it 'recovery'," Mallory said, getting to his feet. "I think 'closure' is a trendy term for it, as well."

Parnell showed his first trace of a smile since they'd arranged for Hunstetter's bail. "Do I smell something shitty?"

"It might just smell like Victory," Mallory told him as he held the office door open. "Want me to hum a few bars for you?"

In the offices of MAURICE BATTLES: BAILOUT MF, the sole proprietor leaned on his desk, his smoky features perturbed. The grizzled mid-ager in western togs, boots, and feather-cockaded Stetson Sturgis wasn't concerned at all. Nobody called him anything but Oakley, and nobody knew him to be anything but serious, cagy and on the ball. He wasn't big or bulgy with muscle, but projected an air of Can Do. With a side order of Don't *Even* Fuck With Me. He shifted a square toothpick to the other side of his mustache and said, "So the geek no-shows and you're on the hook for six million? That's rough. You might have to cut back a little. Drop the country club, the college fund."

"And they say you got no sense of humor. Course it's all laid off. But still."

"Let me guess where that layoff is. Nastiest surety firm west of the Pecos?"

"I think of them as the hungriest. But if you fail to fetch me this asshole back, my premiums gonna hit the moon. All 'insured' means is 'pay us off on time', anyway."

"And they'll come after your fee, won't they? Shit, half million bucks? Grab it and run to Belize. Cuba, somewhere. Blend in, learn the mambo."

"Yeah, sure. Get some hard-on like you come after my ass. Ain't cash anyway: it's a lien on a house. His ex is gonna be *so* pissed.

"That'll teach her. Divorce the guy *after* the embezzlement. Mo, why'd you write this piece of shit?"

"You familiar with a cat name Mallory? Our local gift to the statehouse? Came made me an offer. You know the kind."

CHAPTER FOURTEEN

Even at twelve power, the little blue RC plane three hundred yards away didn't exactly fill the view of the binoculars Bogart had looted out of that ski lodge in Taos four years back. But you could see its prop was spinning, because you couldn't see the prop. The little flivver shuddered, then started bumping forward over the crusty lake bed. "You'd better get if off the ground quick or it's going to tip over and break the prop."

"Don't ever talk to me about flying anything, shithead," Flathead snapped with a noticeable conviction. "I remember your pilot skills.'

"Hey, at least I can do take-offs. You were the one puking and crying and shit."

The two bike bums stood on a slight, scrubby rise. Bogie leaned forward, peering into the binocs, while Flatty manipulated a shoebox-sized radio console with twin joysticks and a yard of telescoping antenna. In the distance the sky-blue plane stumbled along, straightened out as it lightened, then shrugged the surly bonds and buzzed towards the wilder blue.

"You're going the wrong way, dork!" Bogie was having trouble seeing the diminishing plane against the same-colored sky.

"Settle down, Doris. I got it."

And sure enough, with a sunflash of its taut wings, the little plane banked prettily and fell into a flightpath straight toward them.

"Yeh, cool, here it comes!" Bogie was delighted as the radio flyer headed towards them, its propeller a shimmering disk. "Hey, careful, now!"

The plane accelerated, screaming right in on them, the mosquito whine of its tiny engine dopplering as it picked out Bogart as an obvious target. He juked left, then right, then broke into a run, but had to belly-flop into the clay dust as it buzzed right over his scrabbling head.

He jumped back to his feet and threw the binoculars at Flathead. "*Fuck* you, you showoff prick!"

"I still owe you, asshole."

Twiddling the controls, Flathead looped the plane, circled it around their knoll, then brought it down, skipping across the sand towards them. It bumped, a wing caught, and it tumbled almost to their feet. Bogart, his anger typically forgotten, was delighted. "Beautiful, man. Way to fly!'

He snatched the plane up, opened the fuselage, and pulled out a little baggie of pre-rolled reefer. "This is definitely the way to go."

He lit slid a joint out of the airborne bindle, lit it up, and inhaled deeply.

"We could do it at night, easy," Flathead said. "Put a little LED on the ass end."

Bogart took a deeper drag, holding the doobie while examining the tail end of the plane. "Not enough payload, though."

Flathead reached for the joint, but Bogart hit on it again with deep relish.

"Ever wonder why everybody calls you 'Bogart'?" Flatty asked, rhetorically.

"Hey, give a dog a bad name."

He snatched the joint, not without some finger struggle, and took a big hit, himself. "We're almost there."

"All we need is a bigger plane."

"And where would we get it? This was the biggest RC plane they had at the shop and that kid said..."

Bogie shrugged and tried to angle on getting the smoke back. "We could talk to the Mongoose."

CHAPTER FIFTEEN

Mallory and Parnell stepped out of the back of the Battles bond shop, followed by the man himself. A parking lot behind the single-story office was hemmed by taller buildings on both sides and a sagging chainlink fence at the alley. There were several cars in the lot, most of them the sad kind of cars with repo stickers on their windshields. But back by the fence was a powerful, understated old Plymouth Fury, and they headed towards it.

"Mister Oakley what you'd call kinda high power," Battles was saying. "I only work him on big stuff." He shot an eye at Mallory. "Or weird, shitty, blow up in your face stuff."

"But he has a good track record, reputation?" Parnell asked, again. It bothered him that he hadn't been able to come up with anything on Oakley except license records. But of course, this was a guy who traced people for a living, so he'd know how to stay fairly traceless.

Battles smiled to himself. "Want a little anecdote? Might shed light on the picture?"

It had certainly defined Oakley in Battles' mind ten years ago. Dead of winter, come out of his office, here's Oakley in his lined gloves and shearling jacket, standing over there by the Fury. Been two weeks since he'd handed him the paper on that creditcard-jacking fool, but here's the man, right here. "Took you awhile."

Oakley shrugging, "Ended up going all the way to Portland. Mister Criminal Genius was hiding at his sister's place."

Battles peered in the back windows of the Plymouth, the Plexiglas shield from its squad car days still in place, no knobs inside the doors. "Yet, I'm not seeing anybody sitting in there."

"Cause you don't know where to look." Oakley popped the trunk and both of them looked at the folded, shackled body of the bailjumper. Who rolled his eyes pitifully, but spoke not a word.

"Holy shit, you really crammed him in there."

"Might be a little tough wedging him out, all right. It was a long drive."

"Yeah, but... how'd you get him out to, you know, take a piss?"

"If I'd wanted him pissin', I'da watered him."

Now that was worth a stare at the man, then back at the compacted fugitive. "Christ's *sake*, Oakley!"

"Uncooperative."

"Surly, I suppose. Obstructive."

"Recalcitrant. I'll pry him out while you're cutting me my check."

Well, that little tale was an interesting insight into Mister Oakley, all right. Parnell peered dubiously at the manhunter through the driver's window while Battles stood by, bemused. Oakley wasn't taking an ounce of crap off these sharpies.

Telling Parnell, "What do you want, a resume? Endorsement contract? Where do you even come into this situation, for that matter?"

"It's extremely important to this city that you recover Mister Hunstetter..." He was interrupted because Mallory, standing on the passenger side, had laid his briefcase on the hood, and leaned down to the window to say they just wished him luck. He gunned the 440 Hemi engine and a savage twist of torque shrugged the case off onto the ground. Oakley glared as Mallory motioned apologetically and bent to pick it up. And reached quickly into the wheelwell to snap a magnetic homing device on the inside of the fender.

Oakley grimaced at Battles, who spread commiserating hands. Then he pulled forward, banged fists with the husky bondsman in passing and glided out to the street.

Battles watched him turn and drive off, then said, "The game's afoot, gentlemen. I'd bet heavily on Oakley."

Parnell treated him to an oily smile. "I know better than to bet with you, Maurice."

Battles watched the two politicos walk away, muttering under his breath, "Better than betting against me, asshole."

At the street, Parnell looked back at Battles, who hadn't moved, then at Mallory. "I really don't think we can work with this Oakley character."

"No need to," Mallory replied briskly. "I just got his number for the ever-congenial Mister March."

Referring to the same Mister March who grimaced from a devil's face: his eyes bulging open, tongue extended, eyebrows hauled up his forehead while screaming a Japanese syllable. He stood in front of a mirror as he did this, his tight, muscled torso quivering with isometric tension. Tight-skinned, hard-eyed, and close-cropped in his late twenties, March was pretty evidently a dedicated, butt-kicking badass of the first water.

What he saw in the full length mirror in his livingroom/dojo, a sight anybody could view if their luck ran that bad, bore that out in spades. Wearing only a black jockstrap, he moved his buffed, hypertrophied, combat-ready bod through a series of ominous poses, concentrating on symmetrical comparisons. A genuinely scary guy.

In a scary room. And not just the martial arts striking bags and equipment, or the definitive collection of exotic and businesslike weaponry festooning the walls. All those Italian scatterguns, Israeli machine pistols, Russian and Brazilian assault rifles; all those daggers and katanas and ninja doodads. But mostly the scary thing was March himself. Obviously a guy who is heavily, deeply invested in the advantages of killing people and taking pride in looking good while doing it. He broke off his grimacing session to grab a vaguely military looking phone done up in black and olive drab and gave one of his typical laconic responses. "March."

He listened, drumming fingers on his bulletproof pectorals, then said, "I remember you."

Then, "When?"

Then, "Where?"

He nodded, said, "Tomorrow afternoon, there. Have cash." He set the phone down and stood still for a moment, centering his homicidal energies, then spun, delivering a devastating kick to a heavy striking bag.

CHAPTER SIXTEEN

Bunny's eyes popped open to the night. She was immediately awake, but lay on her right side, a spray of hair across her eyes, Coles forearm warm across her waist. There were no lights in the house, so she could see right through the wide doors, across the patio where the hammock hung flaccid in the moonlight like a large-caliber spider web. She could hear the boom/lull of the surf as if it were right outside the door, the castanet clicking of the palm husks. She wondered why she was awake.

Then she knew.

She flipped over and grabbed Cole by the ears, shaking him awake. He came out of a deep post-coital sleep instantly, his six-shooter in his hand from out of nowhere. He looked into Bunny's eyes from a distance of a few inches, and relaxed. She spoke low and soft, but he knew he'd better listen up.

"Just promise me one thing, my beloved simpleton." She released his ears and trailed her hands down to stroke his throat and chest. "If we're out there again, and they start shooting at you, leave the damned money and get your ass out of the line of fire. Will you just do that for me?"

Cole kept his face serious as he said, "Cross my heart, hope to die."

He wasn't set for the steely force she replied with. "Don't you say that!" Her gaze glittered hard on his face, then softened as she murmured, "Just promise me."

"Well, I was always told I was a promising young man."

That was apparently good enough. Mollified, Bunny snuggled back into sleep. The gun was

65

suddenly gone and Cole slid his hand down her waist to draw her in close to him. He inhaled her hair, breathed the bouquet of her throat and shoulders. He leaned close to her ear and whispered, "Promise, Honeygirl."

She smiled in her sleep, rolled back against him. He watched her for awhile, matching her breath, trying to match her heartbeat. "Cross my heart."

CHAPTER SEVENTEEN

The Mongoose's desert-rat hole-up wasn't any cleaner or better-organized than Bogart and Flathead's digs, but it was a whole lot bigger. A clutter of Quonset huts and Conex containers, their metal skins writhing in the heat waves that cooked off them under the merciless sun, made a very vague circle around an abandoned pumping station complicated by rickety outbuildings, scrapwood lean-to's and various outbuildings of no evident purpose or plan. The grounds were littered with wrecked jeeps, cannibalized half-tracks, assault vehicles in varying states of assembly, even the picked-over bones of grounded antique aircraft. Bogie stared around, fascinated as usual, while Flathead talked to Mongoose, a scrawny grease monkey with a somewhat weaselish look. The Mongoose was working on a rather menacing piece of ancient ordinance, fiddling it with an exotic spanner which he often waved around to punctuate his analyses of various situations. He wore grimy jeans, wind-sanded Army boots, and a sleeveless "colors" jacket opened to reveal several tattoos the guys had never been able to fully work out, but seemed to have a lot to do with sex, drugs, and armed assault.

"Shit, 'Goose'," Flathead was saying, "Why don't you build this stuff before you sell it?"

"Some assembly required," he said in his usual bored tone. "Batteries not included. There are people who put together cheap plastic models of war ordnance as a hobby, you know? Nobody gives them any shit about it. So happens, I prefer the real thing."

"In the real gunk," Bogie bitched. "Why do they pack all this cool stuff in that fucking Cosmoline, anyway?"

"This shit's surplus. From like Korea. Spanish American War. Eighteen twelve. Whatever." He put down the spiteful little device and walked away, motioning for the bikers to follow him. He led them through a maze of crates and boxes heaped up like the last act of Raiders of the Ark. "If they didn't grease it, it'd be all rusted out. Besides, it's the factory packing. New in the box. Should be worth extra to collectors. And you snivel about it."

"I hate that goop," Flathead told him, backing up Bogie.

Who yelped, "*You* hate it? Who had to put those fifty World War Harleys together? We still got a few around, I think."

"See?" The Mongoose said, "Collectable." He found what he was looking for in the big encrusted pile of crates. Reaching up with his pre-modern wrench, he tapped two particularly big ones, their wood silvery from years in the sun, the heavy stenciled Army-ese faded. "Here you go. Only two left. Genuine Grade A, government-inspected, RCATs."

Bogart stared at the crates. "What're R cats?"

"Cats R grown up pussies," Mongoose explained. "Acronym for Radio Controlled Aerial Targets." Not trusting Bogie's reading ability, he pointed to the stencil that read, TARGET, AERIAL, RADIO-CONTROLLED, ONE EACH.

"Idea was," he said as he swatted at a wasp with his proto-wrench, "They'd fly these things around, see if they could shoot them down with guided missiles."

Flathead, never a fan of governments in any size or form, shook his head. "What a fucking waste."

68

"I think I mentioned the word 'government'." He grabbed a manifest stapled to the wood, the 1950's staples disintegrating, and handed the stiff yellow sheets to Flatty. "They were really wasted sitting in that warehouse up at Fort Bliss."

That got Bogart's attention. "You got access to Ft. Bliss? Could you get Nikes or SCUDs or anything?"

"Well, it's more like I got access to Juarez, you know what I mean? Look, you wanted a bigger RC plane, this should do you. Unless you want one of those unmanned stealth CIA fuckers. Which are not in stock at the moment."

"We'll take 'em." Flathead was a little dubious, but it made as much sense as anything else they'd done so far. "Discount to the trade?"

"Oh, but of course. Factory financed, nothing down, no payments ever. Free fill-up. Bring the family in for hotdogs. Tell you what, I'll throw in a gallon of this new thinner I got, sorta dissolves the Cosmoline. Sorta."

CHAPTER EIGHTEEN

He had a desk and terminals in his double-wide in Refugio, but Oakley's real office was where he sat sipping sorry coffee and poking at a keyboard extending from his dashboard. The passenger seat of the Fury had been replaced with a fairly fancy computer rig, fax printer and several radios of different bandwidths and legality. He watched data slide past on a flip-down screen above his windshield.

"Hey, hold on a minute," he muttered to himself, something he was doing more and more lately, but hadn't worried about it much yet. "Why'd he buy a car three days ago? He already had a car."

He stared at the display, mulling it over between lukewarm sips from the paper cup with little cardboard sleeve advertising the state lottery. "Okay, he's also got a floozy ex-wife. That could account for it."

He punched more keys with his thick outdoorsman fingers. "Could account for a lot of things."

A few more databases and he was suddenly looking at something even more explanatory. Sold by Value Car Rental. Hmmm. So he must have had it as soon as he ditched that Carston idiot at the airport. He minimized the data and stared at Hunstetter's picture from last year's online voters' pamphlet. Alvin might be turning out to be craftier than he looked. Losing Carston at the airport hadn't impressed Oakley that much: he knew who the guy was and could have lost him in a shower stall. But then to just walk out onto the lot and buy a car? Not bad, Alvin, not bad.

70

Returning to the Texas license registry, he scrolled down through some sub-menus and grunted. Only kept that ex-rental two days. My, my. He read aloud, "New owner, Conrad Brenz of McAllen." Now just imagine that; a border town.

Partially tucked into a little copse of cottonwoods and manzanita, the drab Tercel--now without its FACTORY AIR placard--was evidently getting a new life as a pleasure pit. It rocked. It jerked and jumped. It spewed thudding sexual music and the sounds of teen passion from every aperture. Inside, things appeared to be building towards some sort of climax, due largely to the fleshy efforts of Sandy Jo Brenz, a top-heavy, round-heeled blondish teenybopper, abetted by Manny Chavez, nineteen year-old TexMex heartthrob. Interrupted in her intentions by a heavy-handed triple knock on the roof, Sandy yelped in frustration and beat her own fist tattoo on the sagging headliner fabric of the Tercel. Which immediately steadied down, the sounds stopping abruptly. Sandy looked through the driver's window, heavily steamed by the exertions already mentioned, blew her bleach-burnt hair out of her face with a shaky snort, and joined Manny in scrambling for clothing and position.

Still quite *deshabile*, Sandy Jo rolled the window down and looked out into a two inch leather belt with brass rodeo buckle and a broad expanse of plaid shirt with pearl snaps. Beside her Manny protested, "Don't open it, Sandy! Jesus, are you fuckin' nuts? *Pendeja!*"

Sandy Jo leaned out to see who belonged to the broncobuster buckle and saw a strong, bearded face looking down at her with a faint smile. Whoever it was that went around at night knocking on cars of people just trying to mind their own damn business, he tipped his big ol' hat. "Mister," she pouted, "Anybody ever tell you your timing really sucks?"

The old guy leaned down to her with a sort of half smile and said, "My apologies, Miss. Sandra Jo Brenz, I presume?"

"That's right, Mister Man." Her tone wasn't angry, really. She could see guy was old, but a gentleman, and just had an intuition that he was anyway more of a man than that jackrabbit Manny. She was almost flirtatious, saying, "And who might you be?"

"Name's Oakley, Miss Brenz. You got a minute?"

"Well I do *now.*"

Manny just couldn't believe it. The bitch was actually *talking* to this old goat. Ignoring the hot young guy sitting here with balls going blue and his macho going ballistic. In short, "What the *fuck?*" Getting no immediate response, he followed it up with a shrill, "Get out of here, you geezer-ass *cabrón!*"

Oakley leaned over a little more to scan Manny dismissively. That did it. "You got it, you filthy old perv!" Manny yelled, bailing out the passenger door in his undershorts and one boot. He vaulted the hood with feral agility and took an aggressive step towards the old dude. Who didn't even look at him, just raised his arm. Holding a very short shotgun that Manny ran right into, leading with his Adam's apple. His rage noticeably diminished and Oakley kept him pinned there, talking conversationally to Sandy Jo. "Your father said you'd be at the drive-in. Your friends said you might be out here."

Arranging her hair with cute little pats, Sandy Jo said, "Where they wish they were. So what's on your mind, Big Daddy?"

72

Oakley turned to examine the shaken Manny, who found his professionally assessing gaze fairly disturbing. This old *vato* some sort of urban legend serial killer or something? And what's he say? He says, "Did you put out?"

Stunned by that line of questioning, Manny gulped, "Did I *what?*"

"Did you put out?" Oakley repeated patiently.

Sandy Jo was fairly dismissive herself. "Not what you'd call."

Oakley nodded understandingly, then told Manny, "Well, then, I guess you have to walk."

Turning back to Sandy Jo, he said, "Come on, I'll buy you a malt or something."

"Yeah, a forty would go good about now," she answered, a few seconds before sailing a boot and a pair of Levis out the side window.

The Toot'n'Scoot was straight out of "American Graffiti", Oakley was thinking. He realized the place made him happy. He was glad to see there still were places like this: radio-blasting cars sitting around the circular drive-in and occasionally peeling off to cruise The Drag, other cars pulling in full of laughing kids giddy with their own youth and mobility, hand-drawn signs advertising shakes and fries and baskets, even cuties on roller-skates whisking trays of greaseburgers out and balancing them on half-open windows. It was like a time warp to simpler days and he drank it in as he sifted meticulously through the interior of Sandy Jo's brand new graduation gift Toyota.

Her straining cut-offs perched on his Fury's warm fender, she sipped a caramel shake and watched him hunt. "Gimme a clue. Dope, rubbers, pecker tracks? Citrus moths?"

He stood up examining some clear plastic product wrapping. He showed it to her and she looked at it with a little disappointment. For *that* he busted up her seatcover party before she even got her goodies?

"This yours?"

"Could be. Let's look." She checked the cellophane wrapper, then pointed to the price sticker, laughing. "That there's a bookstore. Not a chance."

Oakley nodded, touched his hat to her and moved around to the Fury's door. She didn't get off the hood, just looked at him a moment and subtly stuck out her chest. "Hey," she purred, "Know one good thing about being old? You can buy us some whiskey."

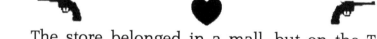

The store belonged in a mall, but on the Texas line had to settle for a tacky mini-mall. Oakley stood outside, waiting while the fey young sales clerk keyed the counter computer, flipped on lights while it warmed up, and glanced around the store before coming back to the doors to let him in. He stepped in past romance cutouts and frenetic displays for teen vampire books. She gave him a look-over, had been aware of him ever since he watched her drive up and open. "You were sleeping in your car when I got here, huh?"

"Nah, just inspecting the insides of my eyelids."

"I've heard of book junkies, but never saw one passed out waiting for us to open. Not even for the new Harry Potters."

Oakley smiled and handed her the wrapper. "This come from here?"

She used a wand on the end of a coiled wire to scan the barcode on the sticker, then consulted the monitor screen. "Not quite here, exactly. But we're a chain."

He nodded. "Does it say what was in it?"

"It lists a twofer deal. Which figures, because we don't normally shrink-wrap books."

"But it doesn't say what books it was or anything?"

"Nope, sorry." She brightened. "But we carry the same package here. Over in the travel section."

This time Oakley's smile was lots bigger. "That kinda figures."

There wasn't much of a line, but it was kind of creeping. Oakley tossed another mini-mart cup of crappy coffee out the window and examined his new package of books. The Spanish-English phrasebook and the paperback edition of MONTERREY ON $20 A DAY. He set the books on the seat and tapped his keyboard. Copies of Hunstetter's picture started emerging from the fax printer, piling up on the floor. The young uniformed immigration officer glanced at the picture oozing out of the printer, gave Oakley the once-over, then stepped back for a very courtly gesture of entry. "*Bienvenido a Mexico, Señor.*"

Oakley replied with equal gravity and pulled forward to pass under the border arch.

CHAPTER NINETEEN

Bogart, greased to his elbows in the putrid, yellowish grease they pack all the cool army stuff in, stood beside a fire made of stenciled crate wood, admiring the fruits of his labor of several days and half the night. The RCAT had a retro-futuristic look, sitting on its steel tubing stand, the fuselage over fifteen feet long, the flat, boxy wings spanning almost twenty. He had painted over the firetruck red finish in matte black, aiding what he kept calling "night ops" until Flatty threatened to break his eight inch TV if he said it one more time. He stroked the beautifully finished wood propeller, as tall as he was and the only component he hadn't had to grub out of the sticky Cosmoline. He grooved on the heads of the opposed cylinders, sticking out of their cowlings and reminiscent of stripped-down street rods and Lafayette dog-fighters.

He stood for fifteen minutes under the gibbous midnight moon, gloating on his handiwork. He was taking lowriding, chop-hopping, and ass dragging to a whole new altitude: he felt that instinctively and stared onto the sleek contours of a new world of his own invention, pulsing in the leaping firelight. When he finally turned away from leching on his new toy, his magpie eye was caught by another ingredient of the crate that hadn't been swathed in loathsome grease; a tight cylinder of actual cellophane, packed full of something that looked like Christmas tree tinsel. His Buck hunter blade flashed out and slit the cellophane--and immediately he was engulfed in strands of tinfoil when the compressed little bale exploded. He held his hands up, drenched in shimmer and fire-glitz and laughed like a two year-old.

He walked around, trailing glitter, laying the coil of foil out on the ground. It was tight at one end, splayed at the other, like a broom. He found the lanyard at the tight end, and tugged it around until he realized it was the handle of a long cone of shredded foil, at least fifty feet of it. Frankly, he just marveled. Then he spotted the tow ring at the ass end of the RCAT and things started to fall together. He quickly located an aluminum carabiner clip amid the drifts of junk around their tent and hooked it all up, smiling in creative delight. Which turned to disappointment in a hurry: here he was standing at the apex of a gigundo cheerleader pom-pom of reflective glamour, and it was just laying there. But, once again, the light dawned on his sleepless, dope-logged mind and he sprang into action.

He set up the radio console by ear; extending the telescoping antenna from the boxy black housing, fingering the switches and joystick before inserting a twelve volt lantern battery. At that point--and very uncharacteristically--he picked up a tan military manual titled with a thirteen digit FM number, and started to read, tracing the words with his moving finger and lips.

It took only two beers worth of skimming and reading to give him the answers he thought he needed, so he flicked a few switches into proper position, dead-centered the little Bakelite joystick, and stepped over to the RCAT. A few checklist moves inside the engine compartment, a quick activation of the chrome switch protected by a snapdown cover on the cowl, and he was ready to address the smooth, insinuating curvature of the hard maple prop--and thus the workings of the engine itself.

He stroked the prop almost lasciviously before moving into a position where he could get maximum leverage, then lovingly positioned his hands and jerked his full weight down on it. The engine had never turned over before, so it took a lot out of the stumpy biker before he heard a few dieselly coughs, then a half-hearted growl, from the little engine. Then it fired, faltered almost long enough for him to clutch the prop again and get crippled, then jounced into life. It settled down quickly, spinning at a lazy idle. Bogie glanced back at the cone of foil, which was shimmering in the propwash, but not really moving. A comet trail of while *caliche* dust feathered off into the desert, fading to black as it escaped the circle of firelight.

He had it figured out now, by God. He skipped over to the console and dialed on a few more RPMs. The little aircraft strained forward somewhat on its stand, but stayed put. Behind it, though, the propwind lifted the tinsel and whipped it around; a stallion tail of sparkle writhing in the flicker of reflected fire. Unbidden, Bogie burst into heartfelt applause. This was just so beautiful, man! Showing some really major, totally bitchin', ass and no two ways about it.

His rapture was interrupted when Flathead, resplendent in stained boxers, a tanktop proclaiming, "We've got a lot in common: I fucked your mother, too," and an old Marine Corps blanket, blasted out of the tent to investigate the dreaded sound of an aircraft engine in the hands of Bogart. Not a happy camper, either.

"What the *fuck* are you doing?" was his cordial greeting. He saw the hula-dancing foil skirt and stopped, gaping. Even to a man accustomed to Bogart's fancies and vagaries, this was a novelty. He turned his eyes back to his partner, more stunned than pissed.

"Came with the kit, man," The Boge announced proudly. "Should look *totally* cool when it flies."

Flatty had to shake his head three times, hard, before he could address the situation. He was almost calm when he said. "It's so radar can spot it easier, you drooling hemorrhoid."

"Oh." That took some wind out of his sails, all right. Flatty was basically okay, but a real wet blanket most of the time. "Yeah, I guess that makes sense."

"We're trying to be transporters, fool. Not targets." When Bogart looked at the gleam dance of the spotting chaff, trailing white powder off it like smoke from a gleaming cigarette tip, his lip curled unhappily and Flatty knew he was going to have a tantrum against giving up anything so shiny, useless, and, he had to admit, really cool-looking. So he stomped over and snatched the console. Pushing Bogart aside, he fingered the switches, looking for one marked, "Turn this sucker off, *now.*"

That was a bit much for Bogie, who kicked him in his narrow ass and grabbed at the console. "Screw you, Mom. I just built it. I got a right to play with it."

Which was exactly what Flathead feared, so he reached for the console again, trying to elbow Bogart away from it. They scuffled for possession, with rapidly escalating levels of violence. Bogie maintained possession of the radio unit, in spite of some nasty shots to his bulging midriff, but was having trouble with offensive moves, since holding it limited him to kicking the bony shanks of a sparring partner too quick and experienced to give anybody a free boot at his nutsack. When Flatty reached in to grab his beard, his thumb sliding into his mouth and wrenching at his cheek, the Bogester flared into true anger, however, and slammed him with the console. That backed him off a step, allowing for a full two-handed sweep with the metal housing, which impacted the center of body mass, switch side down. Immediately the RCAT revved up drastically and departed the stand with a clatter. It dragged tail, zigzagging and fighting for altitude. The tinsel drogue flapped past the dueling bikers, slashing them both with a sirocco of sheen before blitzing off into the night.

The bike bums stood frozen, staring after a bustling circle of gleam, hearing the pipey little two-stroke buzz steadily out of earshot. They looked at each other, dumbfounded, then immediately resumed their battle for control of the remote.

The circular universe of the radar screen, rotationally swept in a biochemical green, was divided by a dully glowing red line indicating the border between the United States and Mexico. Eyeing that line from a fairly uncomfortable plastic seat that had cost tax-payers seven thousand dollars, Specialist Fifth Class Marvin Babson pondered, Which side is worse?

Whatever reasons anybody might have not to like Texas--and you hear them all the time, especially in the world inhabited by Sp5 Babson, a black Muslim and fan of the Washington Redskins--they were negligible compared to his global, multi-national perspective on the issue.

It had played well on all the news shows and columns, everybody all fired up about how wonderful and just, by jingo, jolly it had been for NATO to loan AWACS planes to the U.S. for the border "war". Don't even get into the whole thing of NATO "loaning" us our own shit: point is, it meant flying out of Lackland AFB instead of Germany. Germany! A black American phony-jazzplayer's wet dream. All those little frauleins just fascinated to find about the legendary properties of the black male in action. And maybe a few Swedish mamas, as well, even more curious and uninhibited about giving that curiosity full rein. And Swedish girls were just about Marvin Babson's favorite living organism. Not that those Stuttgart chicks were anything to kick out of the sack.

But that just wouldn't have done, turns out, to leave ol' Starvin' Marvin over there buried up to his cockring in sweet blonde fuzz. Lordy, no; they just hadda ship him over to San For Crissakes Antonio flying over god-forsaken, fraulein-free roadrunner country in jumped-up 707's out of Lackland AB, directing a bunch of bonehead rooks from the Air Guard out of Nellis, with your occasional hard-on from Homeland Security to brighten the outlook. Sitting in a noisy, vibrating echo chamber smelling faintly of light oil and ozone, around a bunch of other enlisted men who were bored out of their minds and didn't smell all that great, either. There was no justice anywhere. And most exceptionally not anywhere along the little jagged line on his scope. There was, however, suddenly a "bogie" on that scope. A weird one. The AWACS radar systems, which are egghead sorcery that compares to ordinary civilian radar much like a nuclear reactor compares to some jungle-bunny's campfire, are bred and calibrated to detect, identify, and point an accusatory and often deadly finger at extremely subtle flying phenomena. Yet they could make very little out of this blip which had popped out of nowhere a short distance on the Mexico side and was resolutely headed north. Babson stared and blinked. Under his breath, he muttered, "What the *hell* is that?"

He spoke aloud into a microphone. "I've got a bogie, six clicks south of the border. It's a weird one."

The voice of the unit C.O, Lt. Waring, came on, bland and supercilious. "Heading and velocity?"

"Twelve point fiver. Hundred and sixty."

"*One* hundred sixty?   Okay, so it's small craft. Probably running in beaners."

Suddenly the triangular blip (now abruptly back under the guidance of Flathead, while his partner spit out some blood and charged back at him) changed course, jittering erratically.

"It's too big, Sir. At least twenty yards long. No wings. Looks like a nose cone. Shakin' all over."

Waring's tone lost some of its superior detachment. Presumably he was looking at a screen now, too. "Jesus, what *is* that thing?

Another voice cut into the electronic conversation, unknown to Babson, but obviously ranking. "We'd better find out."

"Entering U.S. airspace," Babson intoned," Exactly right... now."

"Find out" translated into a Texas Air National Guard F-16, cuttingest edge in the wars on drugs, terrorism, and wetbacks, scrambling up from the runway at Laughlin AFB, screaming off the night runway with the avid intentions of a hotshot young pilot looking for what he'd been trained for: a kill. At Mach 1.2, it took the sleek fighter almost no time to zip from Del Rio, Texas to the area that bleeped so luridly on the AWACS oscilloscopes and increasingly the jaundiced notice of Homeland Security. It streaked through a virtually featureless black sphere,

82

a few clusters of lights below, a fuzz of border settlements off to the South. But...

"There's nothing there." The report was in the blasé, mechanical "jet jock voice", but a little peevishness could be detected. Where was the potential killee hiding, anyway?

The Flight Commander's voice was not featureless at all, but had little to say more helpful than, "Negative. Highly present on my screen."

Laconic in Post TomCruise Pilot Mode, the reply came back, "Mine, too. But no visual." After a pause, he said, "Conical, slow-moving, no lights, no visual, no radio response."

The FC made a quick decision. "Buzz by, drop flares."

Bogart had wrested the RC console back momentarily, but Flatty snatched it when he was distracted by the swooping roar of a jet fighter a few miles to the north. He held it without moving, though, staring in awe as three lights burst on in the sky and started a slow descent, rocking on their little parachutes, sputtering out a red glow in the night.

Getting a glimmer of what that meant, he twiddled the radio controls frantically. Bogart clawed at the console, desperate to save his baby, but the taller Flathead held him off with a straightarm, attempting a U-turn in international airspace.

On the radar screen, the bizarre blip turned slowly back southward. "Object has reversed direction, heading one seventy-nine, eight," Babson flatly stated, then immediately corrected himself. "No wait, it's heading east now. My guess? Drunk Martians."

Lt. Waring, no sense of humor, proclaimed, "Stealth terrorists."

In the tauntingly empty sky, headphones clipped out, "No response or contact?"

"Negative," the pilot replied, getting sick of all the negative. "Sill no visual at all. Scope shows it turning back south."

There was a pregnant pause, a deep breath, then the Word came, strong and clear. "Strafe that fucker. See if he responds to that."

Flathead and Bogart had stopped fighting over the console, since it was now obvious that flying fast, low, and southward was the only option at that point. Then they heard a burst of big-bore automatic weapon fire from the northeast and cringed. Panicked, Bogie made another grab for the console, leading to Flatty biting his upper arm. They were immediately on the ground, rolling around, nipping and gouging.

"Scope shows evasive action," the Commander's voice came over the earphones. "No response or visual?"

"Negative." The pilot definitely pissed-off now. He finally got to actually gun something down, and it didn't *do* anything.

"Okay, then," the Commander snapped. "Seek some heat."

"Fox Two", the pilot rogered, and thumbed off the most dramatic rebuttal in the sleek warhorse's arsenal.

The bikers stopped struggling again, this time in awe of the roar streaking across the sky up north. The AIM Sidewinder missiles sounded like a huge zipper loosening the whole sky. Then they found the pitiful amount of caloric count from the RCAT's two little cylinders, and wolfed down the infrared print like twin sharks after a bleeding mackerel. The Harley Boys were treated to rockets' red glare, followed by bombs bursting in air. A fairly spectacular explosion, even from their remove. As the glare faded, and they could picture their smuggling gizmo converted into a gentle rain of fragments and glittery confetti they turned to stare at each other.

"Wow!" Bogart whooped. "I told you it'd be cool!" He tried a move on the joystick, but was rebuffed.

It's gone, you shithead!" Flathead yelled. "They saw your stupid Christmas tree and blew it up."

Incensed, Bogie glared northward. "Those *bastards*!"

"Oh, sure, blame America first. So you get to build the other one."

"More fucking Cosmoline," Bogart moped. Why couldn't he ever keep anything cool for himself?

"I'll give you a Cosmoline enema if you fire it up solo this time."

"I didn't break it." Bogie was obviously wounded. "They did. The military industrial fuggin complex."

"If you build it, they'll come. You could break a wet dream, you jinx! Get started on the other one."

CHAPTER TWENTY

Oakley, with a stack of Hunstetter portraits in hand, secured the Fury in a commercial parking lot in downtown Monterrey, including arming a few little surprises not featured on most civilian cars. He approached the attendant and pointed at the car, warning and overpaying him. He showed him the picture, but got only a headshake. He walked to the street talking into a cellular phone, paused at the sidewalk, then turned left.

Three hours later the attendant was washing a windshield in a half-assed manner when he spotted this really bad-looking gringo cruising the lot. The guy was wearing all black--tight jeans, body shirt, a multi-pocket ballistic cloth vest, a watchcap--and looked like somebody who might do the final kung fu fight with The Rock in an action movie. Had some little black electronic gadget in his hand and was looking at it as he walked down the lanes of parked cars. The attendant didn't like the looks of that, or of the gringo.

Consulting the device, March walked up to Oakley's car and examined it. He looked around, but ignored the attendant and pulled on some silk gloves and tried the door. The Fury griped about that, but most of its response was cellular signals. Signals jammed by another high tech device in Marsh's vest pocket. The last thing the attendant wanted was to approach this *matón*, but he kind of had to, so he mosied over to accost the waiting March. Who turned an expression on him that rendered him totally meek and agreeable. March pointed at the Fury and raised an eyebrow. The attendant quickly pointed to the street, then left. March nodded and stalked off.

It took less than seven hours, all told.

The hotel Hunstetter had chosen almost at random as a site to hole up while he plotted a way to elude his past but re-acquire his ill-gotten fortune was one of those Mexican commercial hotels that couldn't decide if it was Mexican or "International". It had paper covers on the tumblers and toilet seat, and the end of the roll folded into a little swan, but drinking water was in a green cooler bottle in the hall, and there was no paper prophylaxis on the open carafe on the Formica dresser. Color TV with remote riveted to a swiveling holster on the bedside stand, but a shower divided from the rest of the restroom only by a flimsy plastic curtain. Walmart bedspread, but big thick poly blankets in confused semi-Indian patterns. Tip envelope with English printing, but crappy little hard pillows.

Two of which supported Hunstetter's cropped hair as he lay on the bed in shorts and T-shirt, puzzling at a Spanish language news show that apparently eluded his ability to look up the words in his new bilingual dictionary. But when the knock at the door came, he didn't do that badly. Scanning quickly for the phrase he managed a decent pronunciation for, "*¿Que es?*"

He couldn't make much out of the muffled response, though: "*Servicio de albondigas, Señor,*" means "Meatball service, Sir."

He caught the "service" part and padded to the door in sock feet, still reading from the phrasebook. "*Mande?*"

"Muy importante que registras," came back. "Important", anyway. He gave up and opened the door. Oakley quickly stepped into the room and Hunstetter recoiled, deeply shocked. "Who are you?"

Like that matters, Oakley thought. But said, "Name's Oakley. It's checkout time."

Always a little slow on the uptake, Hunstetter dithered. "I'm going somewhere?"

"Yup. Home."

Within minutes the treasurer, miserable and scared, stood naked with both hands on his head. His luggage had been ransacked and all his clothes were piled on the bed. Oakley closely examined his shoes, then tossed them on top of his clothes. He nodded. "Okay, get dressed. Slowly."

As Hunstetter dressed, Oakley went through his wallet. Unseen, he slipped another transponding disk into a compartment in the wallet. He removed the money and credit cards, then tossed the wallet on the bed and held up the money, cards, and a wristwatch. "You'll get these when you get back. When you get released, anyway."

Hunstetter opened his mouth, started to speak, then thought better of it and shut up. Oakley nodded approvingly. "Good for you, Alvin. I hate all the begging and whining. Your problem isn't with me, it's with the court."

Once dressed and re-packed, Hunstetter stood at the door, Oakley holding him by the elbow. "We're going down to the elevator, taking it to the parking garage, walking over to my car. We run into anybody, keep your eyes lowered and your mouth shut. Do I need to tell you why you'd better do it that way?"

Blinking at him, the unhappy CPA said, "I'd prefer you didn't, actually."

88

"I can tell we're going to get along. Keep being practical and you get to ride in the back seat instead of the trunk." He released him and grasped the doorknob. "Okay, then. On our merry way."

He opened the door and motioned Hunstetter through in ahead of him, just as a black boot came through the door with dazzling speed, catching Hunstetter in the solar plexus, doubling him over, and driving him back into Oakley.

Oakley went with the impact, falling backwards and rolling away from his captive. He came up reaching into his coat but March exploded through the door, stepping on Hunstetter's wrist and spinning a vicious kick to Oakley's head.

Hunstetter scuttled to the closet, holding his damaged wrist against his throbbing abdomen. Oakley slid down the wall in a sitting position, away from the implacable March. He managed to get a gun out, but the black-clad hitman was already pointing an AirTaser at him. He fired and a dart, trailing shiny wire, streaked into Oakley's chest, convulsing him with shock. March smiled cruelly, twisting a control on the Taser as Oakley writhed in pain. Oakley spasmed under increased voltage, just as a second dart zapped into him. Convulsing, he passed out, slumping forward into a powerful kick to the face.

Tossing the Taser onto the inert form of the bounty hunter, March turned to Hunstetter with a feral grin, putting a finger across his lips. Hunstetter nodded frantically. March spun again, kicking the fallen Oakley on the top of his head. Completing the turn, he stared down at Hunstetter and asked, "Are we understood?"

More desperate nods indicated if not understanding precisely, at least compliance. "Then hey," March told him, "Arise and walk."

In the parking garage, March, approached a powerful-looking fourwheel drive Denali SUV holding Hunstetter by the ear, and slammed him into the side. He twisted his arms behind him and slapped on handcuffs. Spinning him around, he popped a golf ball into his mouth and slapped an adhesive dressing over it. Hunstetter stared at him, wide-eyed in terror.

Calmly, reasonably, March said, "We need to talk."

Hunstetter nodded his ass off, imitating a bobblehead dashboard doll on a washboard road. March opened the rear of the SUV, revealing a cage. He grabbed Hunstetter's neck in a "Mr. Spock" hold and applied pressure. Hunstetter spasmed in agony, screaming silently. "What you're experiencing right now is a totally legitimate feeling. Keep it in mind if you feel reluctant."

Hunstetter, overwhelmed by fear and pain, passed thankfully out. March punched him into the SUV, kicked his legs in, and slammed the door on him. "What do you say we go someplace nice and private?"

CHAPTER TWENTY-ONE

Monclavo, a Mexican semi-bordertown, boasted, or at least tolerated, all the usual trappings of a smallish third-rate Third World city: deteriorating concrete buildings, inhabitants mostly women and children, sidewalk vendors choking foot traffic into the hazardous streets, broken down American and Japanese cars, wall-to-wall noise including sidewalk speakers blaring bordermutt rap music to entice customers into drugstores and fabric shops.

Amid the humdrum crunch of humanity and dysfunctional machines an armored car--really not much more than a beefed-up Ford Econoline van-- emblazoned with a BANAMEX logo and a thick layer of soot, sat in front of a large drygoods emporium called, for some baffling reason, "London & Paris". It idled fatly, adding bluish smoke to the overall haze and faintly oozing accordion-pumped *ranchera* music through its closed doors and windows. Two guards in uniformed shirtsleeves and brassy baseball caps walked out of the store, one carrying a money bag and the other a shotgun. Both wore lowslung pistols and kept their free hands on the grips. But were not in the least vigilant, jabbering about the thrilling scoreless Chivas game the night before and that hot number working the store's cashier cage, who dressed like a pious little psalm-singer, but gave them slut-eyed looks. The exact opposite of most *Mexicanas*, and it had them as interested as the pointless soccer game. At the armored van they banged on the rear doors and one of them opened. Just as the inside man reached for the moneybag, a piercing whistle snatched their attention to an approaching red Jeep. Bunny Beaumont leaned out of the Jeep, deliciously desirable in bikini top and ponytail. The leaning did nothing to dispel the guards' immediate and intense interest. She held up a partially unfolded road map, prettily puzzled. And in a very broad accent said, "*Hola, policias. Donde está el station de auto buses?*"

A perfectly valid question, but one that was never answered because Cole appeared from around the curbside open door, snatched the dangling shotgun with one hand, whipping his classic Bisley equalizer against the other guard's head--dropping him like a sack of droppings--and brought it to bear right between the suddenly crossed eyes of the one in the van. The guard who'd donated his shotgun locked up, stared down at his unconscious *compadre*, then took his hand off his holster and held it vaguely raised, never looking at Cole once. The inside guy also stared, immobile, until Cole snapped his fingers and he handed over the bag.

Cole hefted the bag and frowned, then glanced in the van to see only a few flaccid, decidedly not bulging, money sacks. Now it was his turn for a dismayed stare. This was neither his, nor anybody's, idea of a windfall by any stretch of the imagination.

"Come on, Cole!" Bunny hollered from the Jeep. "Get the money and come on, dammit. You hearing me, boy?"

Cole jerked back into his usual alertness, grabbed the security men's guns and shoved them inside the van. He slammed the door shut, jabbed the shotgun through both outside handles, and pocketed the pistols. Bunny started coasting away in the Jeep and he ran after it, diving into the seat, but facing backwards as she initiated her haulass outta town. The van jerked into motion, did a balky U-turn that created a cacophony of horns and insults, and headed after them. Cole, his forearms braced on the back of the bucket seat, peppered the armored van's grill with both of the guards' Llama .38's and it came to a halt so abruptly that a taxi slammed into its rear end. From behind and to the left came the sound of sirens.

Bunny hot-wheeled through the milling downtown adroitly enough, chewing her lip in concentration as she weaved and careened in the Jeep, not always avoiding a little contact here and there. In the wider, less congested streets of the *colonias* she upped her speed and leaned on the horn in case some fool might step out in front of the plummeting CJ-5. Within five minutes she was heading out of town on what was increasingly not an arterial sprinkled with mini-malls and agricultural equipment dealerships, but more like a highway. The sirens were less audible behind them, but just as she hit three-lane blacktop flanked by stark desert and could really put pedal to metal, another siren opened up out ahead of them and got louder fast as it screamed towards them. They saw it almost immediately, a black and white Crown Victoria with lightbars strobing red-blue-red and the siren warbling like a banshee's mother in law. Cole glanced over his shoulder at the approaching cruiser, then turned back to tailgun any possible pursuit.

The Jeep barreled on, absolute top speed for the funky drive train and chancy suspension. The cops hurtled toward them as well, expanding out of the horizon like a hound of harsh justice. Bunny visibly steeled herself for the encounter, thrusting her arms straight on the wheel, hands in the Drivers Ed-approved 2/10 position, elbows locked. Her lip curled back from her gleaming teeth, her eyes widened, her nostrils flared. Very obviously a chick who'd played her share of "chicken" before. And, just as obviously, survived.

She eased into the middle of the road, marking the cops' car exactly, absolutely no give in the finality of her trajectory. Nothing but pure Mexican *macho* kept the *patrulla* in her line of fire until the very last minute. When the driver saw Bunny close her eyes, that male mulishness was replaced a far more sensible attribute: sheer terror. He jerked the wheel in a panic,, praying he wasn't too late, and the two cars passed with an abrasive wipe of wind shear. The cop fought the wheel, trying to recover from a sudden turn at over a hundred and ten, but left the highway and carved up two miles of hardpan until he spun into a whirlwind of dust and broadsided a stand of *cholla*.

Bunny's inner ear gauged the quality of the sound of the siren car blurting by her, opened her eyes, blinked, and shuddered. Her laugh was loud, but not particularly sane. She looked over as Cole turned around in his seat, blowing smoke off the barrels of the two cop guns before sailing them out into the scrub. "Nice job of drivin', Snickerdoodle."

Coming down off her chicken rush, she cut her eyes at him. "But not such a good case of the job, was it? Case of pure blindness, in fact. Complicated by retardation and undeserved self-esteem."

Cole stroked her knee, but she pulled it away. He sighed. "I hate to say I told you we shoulda took a little siesta first, shower after, hit 'em when it cooled down."

She steered, tense and clenched, then relaxed a little. Cole made another try for the knee and she let him get lucky. "You were right for once. Once."

"But, sure, I guess we coulda cased it better.

94

"Twice. Same day. Look and see if there's Jesus and Mary up in the clouds or something."

Cole leaned back and squinted into the depthless blue and piling cumulus. "That one over there kind of looks like a tit."

"And isn't that one over there a re-enactment of Hannibal crossing the Alps with all those elephants?"

"You mean that big old pile of tits?"

"Sure's not a pile of money, is it?"

"Now that you keep mentioning it..."

"Cole we just *lost* money on a robbery."

He considered that irony and shook his head sadly. "Now, where's the justice in *that?*"

Behind them distant sirens sounded and Bunny glanced in the mirror. "Think it's about time we lit out for the lonesome, lover."

Cole stuck one leg over the side door of the Jeep, leaned back in his seat and smiled at her. "Maybe we can find some oasis, fool around a little."

CHAPTER TWENTY-TWO

Where Hunstetter found himself was no oasis, and no fooling, just a basin between two dunes, under a parching sun, floored with a nasty orange dust, and inhabited by the meanest son of bitch he'd ever had the sorrow to run into. He twisted on the ground sobbing in pain, largely because he'd just been shot in both legs. And far from getting any sympathy for that turn of events, he got the demonic March walking over, still holding his huge gun, and kicking him first on one of the bleeding wounds, then the other. Hunstetter grabbed his violated thighs with both hands and screamed like rabbit.

March glowered down at him in disgust. He hated these pale pukes from the slave world, the quailing pussies who thought they ran everything. He'd been fortunate, over the years, to demonstrate to quite a few of them just how wrong that concept was. "Save it, asshole," he commiserated. "Nobody out here to hear you but me and I only want to hear one thing out of you."

"You're demented!" Hunstetter howled. "You're a goddam psychotic!"

"What I am, actually, is impatient."

"Why did you have to shoot *both* my legs?" the embezzler sobbed.

"I admire symmetry. Now start talking while you still have a mouth." He pulled back his foot for another kick, this one symmetrically between the two wounded legs, but whirled, holding the gun behind his thigh, as an old Jeep soared over the dunes, spinning to a halt nearby. He could see a cute chick and some bozo in a cowboy hat. "Great. Is this MTV Spring Break or something?"

Cole stood up to look over the windshield, checking out the fairly odd situation. He cocked his head in assessment and looked down at Bunny, frowning behind the wheel. "One packin', one bleedin'."

Bunny didn't like the slightest thing about the little tableau. "This doesn't look like none of our business, here, Cole."

But Hunstetter, desperation overriding his fear and pain, groveled up on his forearms, face awash with pleading and forlorn hope, and shrilled, "Please help me! This guy is crazy! He's killing me!"

March did a smooth rotation, kicking him over on his back, coming back around to stare at the inconvenient Cole.

Summoning his flagging energies, Hunstetter cried out, "I've got money! I'll pay you a lot of money. Just get me away from..."

March spun out another rotary kick, shutting him up good and proper. He sneered, "Oh, so *now* you suddenly have money."

At the mention of money, Cole slipped out of the Jeep and moseyed over toward this odd couple.

Bunny didn't like that one little bit. "Don't you *dare* get involved in some mess, here, Cole Haskins. This is none of our affair."

March let his gun hand hang free, smirking at Cole in disdain. "Yeah, better do like the bitch says, asshole."

Bunny leaned out of the Jeep and tipped her glasses down to give March an eye. She nodded to Cole. "Okay, you can fuck him off, sweetheart."

March chuckled nastily and raised his hand showing the gun clearly. Cole recognized it as one of those American Eagle automags. Big gun for little dicks, had always been his impression. "Hey, tough guy," March grated. "Remember this?"

Cole moved like a flicker of sunglare, drawing and firing the big Colt in a motion too fast to follow. The huge automatic vanished from March's hand, leaving three of his fingers torn and bleeding. Amazed beyond his experience, he looked down at the gush of blood, then passed out.

"I remember it well," Cole said. "What's your point?"

Hunstetter, having rolled on his side to see if he was slated for rescue or elimination at the hands of a ninja lunatic, stared at Cole, then at March, flabbergasted. But even his unprecedented amazement over seeing the Fastest Gun In The West blow off the Shittiest Captor Ever was compounded when Bunny swarmed out of the Jeep and piled into Cole, smacking him around with both hands as he hunched behind his shoulders for protection. "*Screw* you, Shane!" she yelled. "How many times have I told you not to take stupid risks! Shooting him in the *hand*? My God. Just blow 'em away and get it over with. One of these days..."

Cole looked down, scuffing his boots. "Okay, sorry, Bun."

"Yeah, sure, " Bunny said sulkily. "Don't you sorry me, Quickdraw McGraw."

He snuck a hand around behind her and pulled her in. She resisted, pouting, then melted into a long, hot kiss.

Hunstetter lay there, dirty, throbbing and losing blood, wondering if he was even still alive or experiencing some post-mortem hallucination. Finally he coughed. Cole broke the kiss, which had been getting fairly carnal, and looked him over. "Oh, yeah. Right. Lots of money, you were saying?"

98

Bunny leaned up against him, kittenish, her arm still around his neck. "I think it was, 'a lot of money'."

The pair ambled over to the fallen treasurer, holding hands like school kids. Hunstetter licked his lips and gazed up at them hopefully. "Um, well, yes. The money. Sure thing. It's just that..."

He didn't see Cole move, but suddenly the barrel of an enormous Old West gun was resting on the bridge of his nose, its gigantic bore aimed right into his skull. "Whatever it 'just is'," Cole drawled. "It best not suck."

Holding the .45 between Hunstetter's eyes, he turned to Bunny. "Now is this what you had in mind, Hon? No, seriously, is this safe enough for you? Maybe you should cover him in case I miss."

Bunny's affectionate demeanor evaporated. "You're not qualified to be sarcastic. Just shut up and be persuasive."

Cole nodded and turned back to Hunstetter, hunkered down on his heels to better meet his eye. "Simple deal. You honor your offer to pay us or we leave you alone with Mister Attitude, there."

Bunny stepped up and looked at Hunstetter's wounds, her brow wrinkled with concern. "He's all shot-up, Honey. We need to do something about that. We don't want him bleeding to death on us. Best we should fix up that other shithead, too, I guess.

Cole shot Hunstetter a long-suffering, guy-to-guy look. "You happen to remember her just now slugging me because I *didn't* kill him? Now I've got to save his ass. See what I have to put up with?"

Hunstetter could see all right. Wow. He stammered urgently, "Look, I have the money. Just not with me. That's why he..."

He broke off, staring at March's motionless form. "He just wanted the money. He wasn't taking me back for bail at all."

Cole shot Bunny a look. "Bail, huh? So he's some bondsman you skipped out on? Bet that's how you got the money. And of course it's in a 'safe place'. Am I warm?"

The Jeep bowled across the desert, jouncing a little on ruts and riffles, Cole relaxed at the wheel. In the back seat Hunstetter flopped around a bit, but not enough to keep Bunny from bandaging him up. She tied off another dressing, the last fabric from March's T-shirt, and assessed the patient. "Nothing broken, no major damage, I'd say. You'll be shooting par again in no time. I bet you're already feeling better."

"Much better, thanks." Hunstetter was rather enjoying his invalid status under Bunny's ministrations. "Must have been your fine nursing skills."

"Well," she jerked her head towards Cole, "The Amarillo Kid there gives me a lot of practice."

"Those pills helped a lot, too."

"My last ones, I might add." Cole was less pleased at sharing Bunny's attention. "But we'll sort that out when we get to the money. Which is just exactly where, again?"

Hunstetter shook his head stubbornly. "I told you, I can't just tell you. I'll have to take you there. Listen, how much do you charge for this?"

"For saving your butt?" Cole caught his eye in the rear view mirror. "What would you say the rest of your life is worth?"

Nervously, he changed the subject. "Say, why'd that guy pass out like that? He shot me twice and I didn't lose consciousness. I wish I had."

"Combination of impact shock and hydrostatic pressure. Supreme velocity from hollow slugs and massive powder overloads. I hand-load everything."

Bunny rolled her eyes. "Don't get Mister Biggest Bullets in Town started up."

"Nah, let's get back on that money, a little. Up in the States, you were saying?"

"I had unforeseen complications, you see. I was forced to leave it and run."

"That's another lesson I hope you're paying attention to, Cowboy. Sometimes you leave the money, you run, and you live."

"With some very pricey help from us passing Samaritans. So you're saying we gotta take you back across the border to get paid."

"Well, yes. But if I go back across..."

"We know, sport. They take names and hold grudges."

Cole drove for awhile, mulling that one over. Finally he said, "We might need some special consultants on this one."

"I think we do," she nodded. "Experienced smugglers and border-crashers."

"Well, there's plenty of them up there in Laredo and Matamoros."

"But how many we could trust? One look at Desk Doggie here, and they'll know there's something to shake loose."

"Hey, wait! I know just the guys."

"Guys? Plural? Oh, god, tell me you don't mean the Greazy Riders... No way, Jose."

"Hey, they smuggle stuff. What's the difference between stuff and people?"

"For one thing, dope doesn't have to get there alive."

Startled, Hunstetter jerked his gaze between the two of them. "Wait a minute, now. When you say..."

"Relax," Cole tossed back over his shoulder. "You've seen how negative she gets about everything."

Bunny glared at him. "Those two idiots are probably in jail, anyway. Or someplace even worse."

CHAPTER TWENTY-THREE

Hunstetter hadn't liked the looks of this burnt-out border town, and far less so the exterior of the bar Bunny and Cole led him to, hobbling between them on crutches improvised from slabs torn from the overhead rack of March's Denali. But as they pushed aside the swinging doors emblazoned EL CHINGAZO CANTINA, he discovered that the interior put the façade to shame for sheer border sleaze, menace, and squalor. Bunny looked around with heavy distaste, he took it in more like a trapped bunny.

The Chingazo was mercifully dim, any increase in visibility sure to disappoint even the most jaundiced expectations. The tables were grubby white plastic, leaned on by a mixture of Hispanic badmashes and stray gringos who might as well have worn overalls stenciled with "Parole Jumper". The booths along the wall were even murkier, and the few females in the place were mostly hemmed into the booths engaged in vaguely visible physical interaction. The music was jolting, tuba-driven polka beats with nasal vocals about smuggling narcotics and dealing with faithless women. The bar was lined with disreputable derelicts who scanned Cole with flat eyes, the tottering Hunstetter with understated curiosity, and Bunny with unveiled lust.

"Just perfect for those dirtbag bike trash," she snorted. "Think I'll be safe in the ladies' room?"

"Doubt they get a lot of ladies in here," Cole said, but pointed her towards two dilapidated doors at the rear.

He'd already spotted his potential business associates and tugged the lamed accountant over to a table littered with empty Tecate bottles and other detritus.   Settling awkwardly onto a rickety plastic chair beside a lean hoodlum introduced to him as "Flathead",   Hunstetter   nodded   at   the   usual pleasantries and stared around, appalled. Mustering false bravado, he brightly spoke up,   "Did you find this place in the Michelin Guide?"

The chubby Heck's Angel called "Bogart" for some reason--Hunstetter spotted little resemblance to Sam Spade or Rick--waved an apologetic hand around the sordid surroundings.   "Hey, the Ching's our local office."

"I like what you done with it," Cole murmured, signaling a prowling waitress/hooker for more beer.

Flathead showed some perverse pride in his surroundings, expansively remarking, "Just could be the loosest bar in the entire world."

Hunstetter found that very easy to believe and said so.

Cole finally got the undivided attention of the B-girl, showed five fingers to her, and was rewarded when she headed over carrying five bottles by their long necks. She herself had no neck at all, and no waist to speak of, for that matter. Cole accepted the beers, handed her a bill, and took a pull. "Well, now, I dunno. I've seen some pretty wild spots in my time. Time or two."

"Not as loose as the Ching," Flathead said flatly.

"I wouldn't bet on that one."

Instantly Bogart said, "Hundred bucks?"

"You're on. What's the proof?"

"Thieves' honor," Flatty said.   "You tell me when you decide I won."

Cole looked dubious, and Hunstetter incredulous, but Bogie pointed at the bar, where a pile of tiny plastic vials were piled up in a tortilla basket. A customer, looking in dire need of a transplant of just

104

about everything, tossed a wadded bill on the bar, and *cantinero* motioned for him to take his pick. The wreck snatched a vial and rushed off, already shaking the little "rocks" into a metal pipe in the shape of two lizards fucking.

Cole waggled his hand in the air. So-so, you know. Then he tensed as two cops shouldered through the swinging doors and hosed the place down with authoritative menace.

"Relax there, Sundance, " Flatty told him. "It's Chinatown."

Cole watched carefully but unobtrusively as the heat bellied to the bar and got the full attention of the bartender. The fat one demanded, "Hey, where's Lupita?"

The bartender looked at him a second and asked, "Lupita the cook, or Lupita the whore?"

"The whore, moron. What do I need a cook for?"

The *cantinero* shrugged. "Good point. She should be in that crib over there because I just sold her some crack."

The cop grunted and grabbed two vials, hitched up his gunbelt and headed towards the indicated crib. Cole forked over a hundred dollar bill without a word. Just as Bunny returned, obviously grossed out, from the ladies' room. "Well, that was certainly revolting."

Then she spotted the money that had just changed hands "What was that?" She turned a furious face on Cole: her animation, flared nostrils, flashing eyes and balled fists instantly tightening the watching bikers' pants. "Was that our last hundred, Cole? You better pray it wasn't it our last folding money."

"Little gentlemen's wager, Sunshine," Cole went all sheepish while his sweetheart hit the ceiling;

Hunstetter and the two-wheeler trash looked away out of embarrassment and that male solidarity that crops up in times of tribulation.

"We're down to the cash in our pockets and you're *gambling?*" Her inflection placed proposition betting on roughly the same moral plane as child molestation or sheep-humping.

Cole had known from the first hour he met this girl, scrawny but sexy in her faded denims and hand-me-down work shirts behind the counter of that forgotten filling station with the pathetic tourist zoo, that he was nowhere near her match when it came to talking, so he hung dog as she glared and fumed.

"It doesn't matter how much money you get if you just piss it away like that." She burned off a glance at Bogart and Flatty that Hunstetter felt lucky to have ducked. "*Gentleman's* wager, my achy, breaky ass."

Cole wasn't the brightest bulb on the tree, but he had an instinctive wisdom about certain matters. He ducked his head like a tardy schoolboy and said, "You're exactly right, Honeybunch."

"Not that you've been bringing much in lately." She ramped down from spitfire to sarcasm, as women will do. "Maybe I could take in washing or something."

Cole sulked under her schoolmarm gaze, looking anywhere but into the onslaught of her scorn. Therefore spotting a mean-looking *narco*-gangster in flashy black western wear coming out of a back room, arranging his zipper. Uniform of the trade: dangerously creased Stetson Outlander, boots of hide from some animal that was probably already extinct, bull-roper belt festooned in heavily worked leather cell phone holsters, what Cole had always thought of as a "cocksucker mustache." Four henchmen stood up and flanked him, smiling heavily at his gestures of sexual fulfillment. Cole kept an eye on the bunch as Bunny continued tearing a patch off his butt in front of people he'd hoped to impress into a business deal.

"Flash may do just fine for the short haul, Cole." She continued in the same general vein. "But sometimes you have to grow up and realize it's going to be tomorrow one of these days."

He watched as a very Indian-looking whore, her nakedness not really covered up by a ratty chenille robe, came out of the door behind the gangster, who was still confabbing on his primordial pronging prowess, and grabbed his sleeve. She held out an imploring hand for money. Cole thought she looked like she needed it quick. The *narco* slapped her hand away, sneering. She grabbed him again, begging in mumbled Spanish with a tribal accent, but he backhanded her off her feet. Sobbing, she grabbed for his leg, but he kicked her in the face, infuriated by the laughs of his posse.

Oblivious to this human drama, Bunny was just getting warmed up, "Just look around you. Hanging out in a dump like this with scooter trash. Doesn't that tell you something, Cole? Not that I haven't already told you, but you'd think you could read the writing."

Señor Black Hat stepped over the bleeding, unconscious prostitute and walked to the bar, his flock of badasses pointing and snickering at her exposed crotch and flaccid breasts. He examined the pile of crack vials and nodded to one of his henchmen, who dumped more of them on the pile in the salver. He stretched his hand out to the bartender and imperiously snapped his fingers. The *cantinero* quickly coughed up a big wad of bills, which he accepted arrogantly, without a count, and pocketed it. Nodding to his *compañeros,* he strutted out the back door and turned up the alley with the gunsels at his heels.

Cole tuned back in to Bunny's correctional tirade for a second, stood up with a glare and walked off right in the middle of all that constructive criticism. Bogart was still staring, transfixed, at Bunny, but Flathead watched Cole stomp out the alley door and wondered if it might be a good time to vamoose.

Bunny stared daggers at Cole's retreating back, threw up her hands. "Oh, that's good. That's wonderful. Just wander off and sulk a spell."

She turned to the bikers, who flinched a little under her attention.

"Another beer, Miz Haskins?" Flathead offered.

"Miss Beaumont to you, Captain America," she snapped back. "While awaiting the benefits of matrimony to some no-good Panhandle hotdog."

She continued to fume, but both bike tramps shot looks at the back door as they heard a sequence of five very quick-paced shots outside. They eyed each other and made furtive preparations to get the hell out of Dodge. Bogart quickly drained off the last of his Tecate, but then the door opened and Cole sidled in, calm and casual. He strolled over to the table, sat, and pulled on his beer. Bunny watched him, ready to pounce on any substandard word or behavior. He hauled a big, familiar wad of cash out of the back pocket of his jeans and dumped it into Bunny's open purse. Gave her a look.

"Oh, wonderful," she sighed. "What did you do now? Shoot up some made mafioso kingpin, get us all tortured to death?"

"Damn," the dumbfounded Cole expostulated. "Just ain't no pleasing you, is there, woman?" He stood and stomped over to the bar, where the bartender regarded him in slack-jawed horror and was very fast to grab him some beers.

Bunny smiled fondly at his back, hefting the money. "Gotta admit, he can sure bring home the bacon in a big way." She continued to dote on her guy as he stooped to hand a big bill to the Indian woman, who'd been sitting against the wall moping and rubbing blood off her face with her blanket. She took one look at the money, levitated to her feet and bustled out the door.

"Jesus, Christ!" Bogart had always had a lot of respect for Cole's way with firearms, but was floored, anyway. "That was Ramón and his 'A team'. Cole must be faster than greased pigshit."

"Oh," Bunny breathed soap-operatically, "You have *no* idea." She lowered her gaze, taking in all three men. "You know how guys are always saying they can rock a girl all night long?

"Well, yeah, I guess," Flatty said non-committally.

"Some of those macho, braggart types," Bogart conceded.

"Yeah, well, they can't." Total finality behind that judgement. "But Cole can. Only he's so fast, it only takes him ten minutes."

Hunstetter stared at her, to no degree less mystified than the bikers.

"See," Bunny said carefully, "That's how fast he is."

Everybody else at the table remained nonplussed. She looked at each of them and demurely snapped her purse closed. "Never mind. Just don't ever play stone, paper, scissors with him."

Both bikers stood and went to help Cole in his heavy task of carrying five full Tecate bottles. Bunny shook her head and tipped her beer up for a swig. Hunstetter was openly gaping at her. She smiled at Cole again, then turned back to him. "I'm sure it's pretty much the same as this in all those other think tanks."

CHAPTER TWENTY-FOUR

Oakley cruised the crummy streets of Monclavo like a panther with a grudge, the Fury rumbling slowly along while he consulted the screen of a Walkman-sized GPS device. He was getting warmer. A lot warmer. Vengeance for insult and injury didn't drive him very much. But he generally liked to keep accounts balanced.

Another gringo motorist who nursed wounds and a grudge, March was ostentatiously pissed as he crawled those same streets in his combat-converted Denali, checking his own tiny screen. When he pulled into one plaza, he made a final check and slipped the locator into one of the many special pockets on his black Kevlar vest, hampered and further pissed by his heavily bandaged right hand. He double-parked in front of a bar with an open patio and looked across at a much seedier bar called "El Chingazo". He pointed and a villainous Mexican thug in the passenger seat nodded. He turned to point the dive out to four more heavies in the rear seat. They nodded, too. Lean, hard-faced goons dressed in a mufti that mixed elements of cowboy trash, urban punk, and *narco* chic, they would appear to most people--the laughing, beer-swilling American Harley clubbers in the patio beside them, for instance--as third world street crime, but to Marsh they were simply Day Labor. The very fact he needed help on this job incensed him. But he had a bad hand and, though he had plenty of professional ego, he was not too blinded by it to realize that the guy who'd shot him--then infuriatingly bandaged him before leaving with all his cash, his guns and

111

half his luggage rack--was no ordinary opponent. So gunning him down as painfully as possible would be especially satisfying.

"The Ching" fronted on the plaza with an arcade in front of it, a covered gallery lined with street food stalls, booths selling everything from cell phone time to cheap sunglasses to PlayStation games, and stands for acrylic nails, electrical cord, *narco* and Holy Virgin T-shirts, and condiments. Hookers, corner accordion bands kicking out cowboy laments, shoeshine boys, *chicle* hustlers, and assorted nogoodniks circulated along with the bustle of normal traffic. Oakley's car was parked in a bus zone at the northmost mouth of the square. He stood unobtrusively in the shade of the arcade, keeping a keen eye on Club Chingazo.

He spotted March's car before he even ID'ed the driver and clucked to himself. Why didn't this asshole just get big signs saying, "Hi, I'm Mercenary Muscle"? He watched him get out of the SUV, followed by his new thug detachment. He didn't like the looks of that much, but figured he could deal with it when the time came. The thugs eased out of the Denali, looking around as if up for anything truly unwholesome.

March scanned the Motorcycle Enthusiasts partying on the patio in their gleaming leathers, their pampered dresser Harleys hugging the outside of the divider rail. They looked like the old "you meet the nicest people on a motorcycle" ads and he dismissed them. He gave a longer glance at two grungy choppers leaning outside the doors of the Chingazo, whose nice owners we've already met. What he was especially looking for was a Jeep with the top down, but couldn't see it because Bunny had wedged it into the alley so people like him wouldn't see it. He also

112

missed Oakley's Fury, hidden by the off-duty bus sporting city routes on its windshield and a half-scrubbed-off WESTFIELD CHRISTIAN ACADEMY on the side. He laid out his game plan. They all nodded. Check, *patrón*.

Two of the temp thugs crossed to the patio, smirked at the Enthusiasts, and straddled the hand-rubbed Harley-Davidsons. The motorcycle fanciers bolted up out of their seats, spilling ice from beer buckets, but were pacified by a display of ready pistols and nasty knifes. One thug started his engine, the other pointed a gun at a Wichita Falls dentist in black leathers and was rewarded by a hastily-thrown chain of keys. They fired up the dressers and chugged over to March, who motioned them to block the streets leading out of the plaza.

Oakley watched these preparations and faded back into the teeming shadows of the arcade. The scenario had "OK Corral" written all over it.

March marshaled his troops and marched them across to the Ching, flanked by the two largest ones. He was a pace from the sidewalk when the door opened and Bunny and Cole walked out into the sun-dappled arcade, along with Flathead, Bogart, and the limping Hunstetter. One glimpse of recognition between Cole and March and pistols flashed into view. Cole pushed Bunny down behind a taco cart in the same movement as pulling his Colt. March had his Eagle out almost as quickly and started firing at him lefty, but hit nobody but a few scattering bystanders. Cole was in a crouch, throwing spectacular moves and precision lead. March was moving too fast and erratic to take a bullet but his bookend thugs went down before even clearing their weapons.

Bunny, on her butt behind the taco wagon, kicked Hunstetter's roof scrap crutches out from under him, crashing him to the cobbled sidewalk under the arches. She grabbed him and started crawling down the sidewalk, dragging him along thrashing in panic.

March, caught by surprise despite his planning and superior firepower, retreated towards the Denali, just as its driver's window exploded. Two thugs stood behind it, firing curved-clip assault rifles over the hood and roof. Cole crouched behind an abandoned pirate CD stall and calmly reloaded, then shot the right hand tires of the SUV, but to no effect since they were foam-filled combat tires. Shaking his head with irritation at wasting ammo, he plugged one of the thugs, who spun away behind the SUV, his Kalashnikov wheeling in the air before crashing into the kitchen of the patio café.

Bunny continued her retreat with Hunstetter in tow. She dropped her purse and could see it laying on the cobbles of the sidewalk, open with the money sticking out, and cursed quietly as she manhandled her crippled client around the corner to the Jeep. She stood and hauled him up, surprising him with the strength of her hands in his armpits as she jerked him to his feet, leaned him forward over the rear gate of the Jeep, and shoved him in. He yelped in pain when she grabbed his legs to toss them inside, but all told wasn't displeased to be elsewhere than in the middle of a firefight.

Bogie and Flatty had gotten to their chops, but crouched behind them. Pinned down and unable to move. Cole glanced toward them and got a mouthed, "WTF," from Bogart, but could only shrug. You get these kinda days now and again. The three stayed low, waiting for a break from the continual gunfire.

114

In the alley, Bunny fired up the Jeep and shifted into low, crouching low in the seat. Hunstetter trembled like castanets as she eased forward enough to peek down the arcade and check on Cole and the boys. He caught her eye at once and pointed to a street opening away from the SUV. Then he motioned to Flathead, getting a nod before suddenly launching himself out into the plaza, running like Walter Payton, firing maniacally. March and the three remaining goons opened up a deafening barrage. Bunny, screaming her high school team's battle cry ("CANNIBAL!") stabbed it, bursting through some pottery stalls to barge out into the plaza heading straight for Cole. The bikers took advantage of the diversion to jump on, fire up, and patch out.

Running for the Jeep, Cole spotted Bunny's purse, surrounded by scattered bills and chick stuff, and faltered. She leaned on the horn and he took another long stride and dived in, landing right on Hunstetter, who screeched in pain and shock. The windshield took multiple hits, disappearing in a flurry of glass pellets. Cole vaulted the passenger seat and started firing from behind it as Bunny burned out in reverse, Hunstetter now screaming in earnest. The Jeep disappeared into the mouth of the street, Bunny "chickening" one of the Harley thief goons into falling over as she whipped past. But he was up and after her, followed by the other cycle goon and the Denali blasting on full automatic.

Oakley stepped out from cover, looking after the motorcade. He tugged his hat down, wiped his brow with his sleeve and heaved an exasperated sigh. Sometimes you just couldn't get cuffs on a jumper to save your life. He was opening the door of his Plymouth when he heard a rattle of racket from the plaza, over where the gaping front entrances to a torn-out storefront were blocked by a barrier of corrugated steel. He whistled as the metal bulged and burst out into the plaza, a twenty foot section of twelve foot metal fence tearing out onto the cobblestones like a snowplow from hell.

The pursuit through unfamiliar, twisted streets had forced Bunny to double back, and when she found herself in a wall-lined block, forked between guns to front and rear, she'd slammed through a rickety wooden garage door and emerged into the hollowed-out department store that had once dominated the plaza's commerce. Keeping the pedal down and her teeth clenched, she accelerated into the metal barrier and now carried a big chunk of it out into the plaza. Still wheeling in reverse, and blinded by the "L" shaped fence wrapped around the tailgate, she blitzed around the square backwards, terrorizing people and animals alike. She shoved the fence up against a wheeled ice-cream cart, pushing it around the square while the vendor sat on top of his tins of home-made cream, howling in fear. Bogart and Flathead were right behind her, hotly pursued by the thugs on pilfered Harleys.

Cole, aiming behind them through the de-glazed windshield frame, suddenly yelled, "STOP!"

Bunny stomped the breaks instantly. The fence, without a Jeep bullying it around, flopped down in front of them, standing on the short end of the "L". The ice-cream cart continued on its momentum, careening into a crowd of locals huddled under the arcade opposite the Ching. Unable to maneuver around the suddenly immobile fence, Bogart laid his bike down, riding its skid onto the short portion of the bent fence. Cole pointed ahead, through the empty windshield. "GO!"

Bunny grabbed first gear and jammed forward, pulling off the "L" of metal, which stood there because Bogart and his bike were lying on the short end. Flathead also braked to avoid running right over him, flying over the handlebars to slam into the erect long end of the "L", knocking it flat. And snapping the short end up to lob Bogart up beside him, both bikers lying stunned on the fencing.

The pursuing thugs slammed their cycles into the short end of the fence at full speed, instantly punching both of them out.

Free of the fence, Bunny dashed towards the open storefront. But March was already there in his SUV/gunship, heading through the gap she'd blasted in the fence and straight toward her. She carved a tight, fast curve that brought the Jeep up on two wheels, tires and Hunstetter screeching in harmony, and headed around the plaza with March's gang in pursuit throwing as much lead as they could without getting blown away by Cole, who was becoming increasingly frustrating because everything he was hitting seemed to be bulletproof. The chase circled the square, instigating more picturesque destruction of handicraft and taco stands and further lamentations from the citizens.

Cole kept firing to little effect other than starring the combat grade windshield, Hunstetter kept bawling as he banged around in back, and Bunny continued trying to shake March and his *pistoleros.* She spun and brodied, got chased right back over the fence section. Getting a little sky from blasting off the raised curb, the Jeep skimmed past the bikers lying on the flat long section of the fence, smashing into the vertical short segment. The passage of the Jeep caused the "L" to rock forward into an upright position, catapulting both dazed bikers into the air.

Flathead sailed through a floundering, wailing arch that landed him on an *elotes* cart, ass-first into a huge tub of boiling water full of corn on the cob. He launched out again, yowling like a scalded cat.

Bogart hit a long table lined with overturned chairs and slid along it until his head hit and ruptured a big ceramic bowl full of red *chile* sauce. He was on his feet immediately, painted gory with the pepper sauce, dancing around, and rubbing his eyes while keening, "Whoaowwwwwwwwwwww! This shit burns! Where's my bike?   I'm fucking blind, man!"   He staggered around groping, until he stumbled through the wall of a drink stand and plunged his head into a twenty liter glass jar of liquid floating with strange fruit and diced cactus.

The fence section, having tossed them away, but still empowered by the trajectory of Bunny's Jeep, continued to roll over, tossing up onto the long end just in time for March's SUV to impact it. The ragged metal edge did what Cole's slugs hadn't, slashing into the Denali just above the windshield and slicing back the roof like a dull razor blade. Dismayed, he drove forward another twenty feet, the fence section snowplowing the Harley thugs along in front of it.

Finally free from following fire, Bunny headed for the street opening again, scattering whoever wasn't already sufficiently scattered. The Jeep, battered and peppered but still game, plunged into the street and clumped off to safety on perforated tires, trailing Hunstetter's squeals and groans.

Tearing along the highway on bare steel rims, once again aware of sirens behind, Bunny turned an affectionate gaze on Cole, who was reloading and shaking his head at the sheer perfidy of people who would armor an SUV to the point a body couldn't even shoot holes in it. "You did it, Sugarboy," she beamed. "I am so proud of you."

Cole was taken aback, but not loath to glom a little pride and praise. "Did what? Didn't hit anybody important, lost the money. What we gonna do for a windshield?"

"You left the money, like you promised. And didn't get your unit blown in the dirt from showing off."

"Listen, a promise is a promise, Cutiepants. However distasteful it might appear at the moment."

"I just love you so much I could bust, Cole Haskins. You need to kiss me right this minute."

Cole leaned over for an enthusiastic and extended kiss, accompanied by a certain amount of instability in the motion of the fleeing Jeep.

Watching with trepidation from the back, Hunstetter said, "You people are absolutely certifiable."

"Yeah," Bunny cheerfully agreed, "But we sure can smooch."

"And," Cole added, "Damnwell know how to nasty."

Not a man to lightly abandon his plans for murder and mayhem, March jumped from his disabled Denali, ignored the hick gunmen, and ran to Flathead's chopper. Snatching it up from the pavement, he straddled it, kicked it on, and jerked it around towards Cole and Bunny's rapidly dispersing dust.

Flathead was slumped in a seated position, and majorly dazed, but the sight of this fuckhead jacking his bike motivated him greatly. Leaning over on one bruised buttock, he groaned and fumbled in his pockets. And found the little black car alarm remote. He pointed it at March with a vulpine grimace.

March revved, clutched, and accelerated after the long gone Jeep. He made it about ten feet before Flathead pushed the button on the remote, activating his highly customized preventative measures. March grunted like a poleaxed bullock, his arms vibrating from the high voltage electricity the bike's old magneto was feeding into the grips. And two flat steel rivets strategically placed on the saddle. His hands clasped rigidly by the galvanic attentions of Flatty's idea of theft alarm, he plunged at full speed into a stall hung with fake Aztec motif blankets, wrapping himself in pilly, polymer-smelling synthetic shrouds as he busted out of the stall and crunched into one of the arcade pillars. Released from the clutch of the rogue capacitors, he flopped on the stones on his back, hands still twitching and clenching.

Grunting up to his feet, Flathead limped towards his chopper--the truly significant other in his life. March controlled his tremors, rolled up to his knees in a fancy Kung Fu move, pulled his mega-gun, and pointed at Flatty, his face speaking of terminal intentions. The biker froze in his tracks. So he wasn't going to die on his wheels after all. Go figure.

Except Oakley glided smoothly from behind a *menudo* stall, snatching up an iron skillet off the burner. He stepped up behind March, who sensed his presence and started to bust another cute move. Abandoned of necessity as Oakley forehanded the skillet into the back of his head with a full swing that recalled Roger Federer, thus putting everything out of March's mind while he fell on his face, drenched in boiling grease.

120

He took a step closer, holding the skillet ready for a backhand *coup de grace,* but it wasn't necessary. He wrinkled his nose and shook his head at what the scalding oil was doing to the back of the ninja-merc's head and hands. Flatty shuffled up, dragging one frayed boot. He managed to get the double-barreled sawed off shotgun with handcarved wood pistol grip out of the back of his jeans and point it at Oakley, but without much conviction. Oakley smiled and made a "be my guest" gesture at the bike. Flathead motioned with the shorty and he picked up the bike, rested it on its kickstand and brushed off the seat with a sales floor flourish. He backed away and waved goodbye as Flathead mounted up and popped a wheel getting the hell out of there, Bogart right behind him with his face flushed pink and his T-shirt soaked with Mexico Kool-Aid.

Oakley looked around the plaza, taking in the destruction, lingering confusion, and stunned gazes. "What the hellity damn was *that?*" he asked rhetorically as he moved to the Fury, already consulting his tracer.

As he exited the square, about five minutes before a dozen caterwauling police cars entered it, the gringo motorcycle enthusiasts approached their banged-up treasures, horror and shock writ large on their faces. One of March's thugs moaned, raising his head. One of the Nicest People grabbed up the *menudo* skillet and pounded the offending head repeatedly. His fellow dresser fans found other utensils to treat the other thugs to much of the same.

CHAPTER TWENTY-FIVE

Bunny perched her perfect posterior on a crate, maintaining her aloofness from the surrounding squalor at the bikers' hideout. Hunstetter sat in the dirt, leaning against a device made of car jacks and pallet lumber to be used for compressing bales of herb, fiddling with a pair of wooden crutches so antiquated and bulky they suggested Civil War surplus. Cole hunkered on the heels of his Tony Lamas, plotting advanced strategy with the Bike Bros, who lolled in their ratty nylon hammocks.

"Nah," he was telling them, "I don't think it's such a good idea letting him go off with y'all."

"Not a chance, is what he's saying." Bunny clarified.

"Well," Bogart pondered. "You guys sure as hell can't take him over. You're both still hot as two-peckered billygoats from that..."

Bunny coughed, cast her eyes towards Hunstetter, and said, "No history lessons, please."

"Oh, yeah. But anyway, you can't."

Flathead looked at Hunstetter fumbling ineptly with the giant, corroded wing nuts on the Appomattox crutches and offered, "And he can't cross the desert with his legs shot up. He can barely take a piss by himself."

"That's a complete exaggeration," Hunstetter said, taking umbrage at one more of the insults to his entire organism that had been piling up ever since he lay down in the hotel room.

Ignoring him, Flathead went on, "And we can't just tape him under a truck. I don't see any way."

Suddenly Bogart's chile-flushed face lit up like a tail light. He beamed with yet one more inventive rush. "Hey! No problemo, Bro!"

That unexpected optimism drew curious stares all around and he did a hand move like a magician producing a bunny. "It's RCAT time!"

Naturally, that proclamation left most of his audience in the dark. Cole decided to bite, Bunny figuring he'd regret it. "Yer cat?"

"You're stoned, bonehead," Flathead snapped. "For one thing, there's no room in that thing."

"I beg to differ, amigo," Bogie preened. "I made a few modifications. Kustom Kraft."

"Oh, shit, where's a big wrench for your screwloose fuckin head?"

"Go ahead, laugh," Bogie condescended from the pedestal of his own genius.

"I'm a long way from laughing, dickwad."

"Just like they laughed at the Smith Brothers' airplane and shit." He stalked off around the big tent with afflicted dignity. Still clueless about the whole issue, the rest got up and followed him. Hunstetter brought up the rear, his crutches so short he had to stoop.

Out back--as if their entire bivouac wasn't Outback--Bogie stopped in front of an abstract shape draped in a tarp. With showbiz aplomb, he snatched away the tarp to unveil the glories of the Kustom RCAT Mark II. Many in the audience were awed, others entertained other emotions.

No flat nite-op black on this baby: it was all KandyApple red, except for the vaguely Tibetan black and orange flames that chased back from the protruding engine cylinders. It sported a stepped, two-passenger motorcycle seat on top, flip-up foot pegs at the bottom of the fuselage, and a pair of shoulder-high "ape hanger" handlebars up top, complete with knurled grips, chrome levers, and black leather tassels dangling from the ends. It took a moment for the whole enormity of it to fully register.

Flathead's registration was emphatic. "I'm gotta bust up your idiot ass."

"It's adorable," Bunny cooed. "Do you put in a quarter for a ride?"

Cole was totally sold. He'd have bought one in a hot second. Well, stolen one, more likely. "Holy cats, Bogie! It's a wet dream! You got, like, Bike Rogers here."

Glowing with authorial pride, Bogart swung onto the saddle to demonstrate niceties not immediately appreciated. "See, this lever's gas, this one's the choke. Pull back to climb."

He pulled back on the yoke-shaped handlebars and the flaps on the tail fins lifted, then flapped noisily. "Push forward to dive." Sure enough, when he nudged the bars forward, the rear flaps dropped.

"But how do you steer it?" Cole wondered.

"No controls, just shift your weight."

"You're out of what little fucking mind you ever had," Flathead muttered in a dangerous undertone.

"It'll fly, Bro. I tweaked a lot more horses out of the engine, too. Those Army dingbats don't know shit about performance."

Bunny walked over, eyeing the RCAT closely. She stroked its sleek flanks and looked up at Bogart with grudging respect. Just viewed as a sculpture, alone...

She turned to Cole. "It's completely insane, Baby, but I don't see any other way to work it."

Cole also petted the gleaming target/chopper and smiled. "Think it'll seat five?"

"We'll work out the details. But however we do it, I'm not staying here alone. Or with those bike bozos."

CHAPTER TWENTY-SIX

They were ghost buildings.

Abandoned human services on an irrelevant stretch of blue-line highway. A faded, shot-up sign near what might have once been a Texaco station read, LAREDO - 127 under a Texas-shaped badge for STATE ROUTE 83.

Flathead straddled his chopper, looking back, askance, at Bogart, who was still fiddling around under the raised hood of a revving Chevy Malibu that had seen better days but seemed to run strong enough.

"Just cut the jumpwire and leave it," he said wearily.

The hijacked Malibu's engine stopped and Bogart squirmed out from under the hood and slammed it shut. Turning to Flatty, wiping his grease-smeared hands on his grease-smeared vest, and said, "What if they can't start it again?"

"Oh, I think Haskins might have stolen a few cars in his time."

"Bunny, too, I bet," Bogart nodded. He took two steps toward the idling chopper and stopped suddenly, totally aghast. "Wait a minute. I ride up back? Like some piece of tail?"

"How'd you think we were going to get back?" Flatty answered, "patiently".

Staring at the shame of the rear pillion, Bogart muttered, "I didn't think about it, but..."

"Now there's a surprise." He gestured impatiently. "Jump on, we've still got to get back and bring the lovebirds up to where they jump the line."

"Well... Okay. But don't tell anybody."

"Look, riding on back doesn't compromise your masculinity, all right?"

"Well, okay. But shit." He gingerly cocked a leg over the rear wheel and seated himself behind Flathead, leaning back as far as possible from any suspect contact, his face a mask of distaste.

"Secure in your manhood, there?"

"Just get us the fuck out of here, will you?"

"Right on, man. Oh, wait. Let me..." He shrugged his insignia vest off his shoulders, scrunching it down around his hips, and sat tall in only the grimy T-shirt he wore underneath his "colors". He looked back at Bogie, snickered, and burned off into the night.

Alone at the bikers' camp, Hunstetter sat by an open fire, chained like a dog. As if he could go anywhere. He looked up as Flathead's bike pulled into the circle of firelight, belching a little as the compression slacked off.

Bogie could not *wait* to get off the pillion seat. He jumped off, shuddering, then saw the back of Flathead's T-shirt: IF YOU CAN READ THIS THE BITCH FELL OFF.

"Fuck you twice, you cocksucker!" he screamed, slugging the back of Flatty's head and knocking him off the bike. Flathead came up swinging and they had at it, rolling around on the ground in a wild fracas that terrorized the leashed Hunstetter, who kept yipping in pain from his leg wounds as he scrambled to stay out of their way.

Bunny and Cole crouched behind separate clumps of tumbleweed, watching the searchlight of an official Border Patrol Suburban sweeping the ground. "I told you we should have waited for those morons to come back and bring us to their special crossing spot," Bunny said in a low voice.

"We'da been sitting there next week. It's not a problem. We can walk across the border easy as any Julio can, you notice. If they stole a car, they left it on a road, right?"

"Well, I'd rather be lost in the desert at night, pursued by Homemade Security, than riding behind either one of those yo-yos," Bunny said with conviction. "Now you remember what we say if they catch us out here and question us, right?"

"Bang, bang, bangity, bang?"

"Not funny, Cole. We're hippies looking for peyote and got lost. Okay?"

"Yeh, I really look like some damn hippie."

"Okay, then, we're drugstore cowboys looking for peyote. And be polite. Can you do that?"

It was almost dawn before Cole and Bunny straggled out of the desert and approached the heisted Malibu. Cole looked inside, opened the hood and fiddled. Sparks danced under the hood, then the engine turned over. Cole kept fooling around, staring at the sparks. Bunny leaned her head out the passenger door, giving him a quizzical look. "It's running, Cole. And getting light. Let's go."

Cole, distracted and rather spacey, slammed the hood down, stared at it, then opened it and slammed it again. Looking up at Bunny's amazed face, he gave the open smile of the mentally deficient and said, "Maybe you best drive, Lovedove."

Sliding across the seat, Bunny just had to ask, "You okay?"

"Not sure yet. See, I actually did run across some of that peyote back there, and tried a few out. It seems to be kinda going to my head.

With Bunny sticking to the speed limit and keeping an eye on the horizon and rear mirror, Cole paid respectful attention to the suggestive whine of the Malibu's oversized engine while stoically regarding a neon dance of hallucinatory animation unfolding from the seething colors of the dawn. Continuing what might have otherwise been called his pattern of thought, he said, "Now, see, there's you, then there's me. Then there's this other thing that's like both of us. And I can't figure which one is calling the shots. You understand what I'm driving at?"

Bunny looked across and patted his knee. "Know what, Loverman?" She flipped on the CD player slung under the dash and the car was immediately drenched in steely Texas whiteboy blues. Cole sagged back into the seat, overcome with revelation. "Holy, shit, you're right! This guy is on top of all of it!"

"The gospel according to Stevie Ray."

"See can we find a motel, Cutiepie. This stuff is starting to get interesting."

Bogart, showing signs of recent hard use, sat proud as punch in the RCAT saddle, toying with the grips as the engine revved up and down. Duct-taped to the seat behind him, his Confederate crutches strapped across his back, Hunstetter lolled drunkenly. Both wore old-fashioned goggles and black fiberglass Nazi-style helmets.

Flathead, also visibly battered, watched them with a mixture of foreboding and disgust. He held a bottle of Tequila, almost empty, which Hunstetter was fixated on, smacking his lips a little. "Come on," he slurred, "One more for the road, you stingy ol' dirtbag cycle tramp, you."

"Make it two," Bogart chirped, snugging down his round-eyed goggles.

"Forget it, Bogie. You gotta drive. He's gotta be anesthetized." He stepped over to Hunstetter, who tipped his head back to receive the last of the Tequila down his gaping throat.

"That tastes like shit!" he croaked. "Any more?"

"Would you two get your doomed asses out of here?" Flatty snapped, tossing the empty Jimador bottle out into the dust.

Incensed, the trussed Hunstetter gibbered at him, "What?! Up yours, Roadkill! I'll kick the shit out of your ass!" He jerked around, gave Flathead the finger, which Bogie echoed, then dialed the handgrip all the way over. With a pipey roar, the RCAT sprang off its stand. It immediately plunged onto the hardpack, dragging its tail away like a sick dog. Then, with a resigned shrug, and a few judicious kickoffs from Bogart, it cleared the ground. Flathead watched, astounded, as it struggled aloft.

The little plane zigzagged off into the sunrise, Hunstetter's yell trailing behind it, "Yeeeeehaw! Ride 'em dogie!"

Flathead watched them wobble away, then turned around so he wouldn't have to watch. "You two assholes *so* deserve each other."

Definitely hoping to avoid further attentions from the slings and missiles of the War On Drugs, Terrorism, and Anything Else That Moves, Bogart hugged the ground on his insane flightpath, zipping through gullies, dodging cactus, shooting arroyos. Behind him Hunstetter--who they'd been unable to get on the plane when sober--slopped from side to side, hootin' and hollerin'. Bogie tried some exploratory aerobatic stunts, a couple of which scared the crap even out of himself. More screams and squeals from Hunstetter, who had become a fairly experienced screamer over the past three days. Bogart shouted over his shoulder, "Wanna try a roll?"

"Oh, there's snacks on this flight?" Hunstetter shrieked into the wind.

Bogart got a good grip with his knees and leaned the RCAT into a roll. He was absolutely delighted with the result, even though the moving target dipped a few feet, almost brushing his helmet against some tumbleweed. Hunstetter, needless to say, screamed.

Near the U.S. border, a Mexican *campesino*, dressed in full stereotype drag with his *serape* and *sombrero*, leading the inevitable burro, padded along one of the endless foot paths that cross the desert from nowhere to nowhere. Looking to the North, he could actually see the border fence. Which reminded him: he dropped the burro's line, tugged down the waist of his white cotton *pantalones*, and uncorked a long, languid piss on the pipe organ column of a Saguaro cactus. He was almost drained when a whining roar engulfed him, a mighty wind thrashed his clothes, and a flying buzzsaw chopped the top right out of his sombrero. Shaken, he doffed the sombrero, now resembling a topless volcano, and stuck his fingers through the crater. He looked up and saw that the cactus had also been topped off, ending in a slightly circular cut at the top. "*¡Hijo de la*

chingada!" he exclaimed, and the burro echoed the sentiments with a hiccuping bray.

Beaded with a light spray of cactus juice, the RCAT popped over a bluff and dropped down to skim the surface of the man-made lake called La Amistad Reservoir. Scanning the flat, windless water, Bogart spotted what he was looking for, hauled out his folding Buck knife and reached back to where Hunstetter quailed away from the blade. He slashed the duct tape, freeing the accountant to move about the aircraft, and gripped the knife in his teeth. He looked around at his passenger, who laughed heartily at the apparition, "Yeah! Yo, ho, ho, matey! Let's go pirate some pillage."

"Ready for another roll?" Bogey asked around the blade.

"You betcha, buddey. How about some roasted peanuts? More of that Tequila?"

Bogart swooped downward towards the blue mirror of the reservoir, and threw his body to his left, flipping the RCAT upside-down. Keening in terror and delight, Hunstetter fell like a stone into the water. Lightened, the RCAT popped higher as Bogie flipped it right-side-up and blasted away.

Squawking and splashing, a breathless Hunstetter dog-paddled in the water, continuing his mastery of the scream. A boat horn tooted behind him and he thrashed around for a look.

A very classy cabin cruiser, all waxed white fiberglass and polished brightwork, was heading towards him, tooting once again. He couldn't decide whether to swim evasively or dive, so he flopped around some more, blubbing in consternation. The boat turned broadside, or hove to, or whatever stolen yuppie boats do on fake desert lakes, to reveal Bunny, radiant in bikini and straw hat, at the wheel. She brought the boat around nicely, to present Hunstetter with the stern. Which bore the boat's given name, GRAB HOLT, out of Del Rio, Texas. Shirtless in cutoffs, boots, Stetson, and aviator sunglasses, Cole stood on the rear deck with a longneck beer in one hand and a loop of ski rope in the other.

"Don't make me have to rope and tie you," he called to the waterlogged accountant. "My rodeo skills are a bit rusty these days."

Hunstetter was appalled, a state it was getting harder and harder for him to achieve given recent events. "I can't water-ski, you cretins! My legs are shot. I'm a casualty, goddam you!"

"Ain't water-skiing," Cole reassured him. "We're trolling for water moccasins."

The water fluttered as Bogart blitzed by on the RCAT, yelping. Bunny grabbed her hat with one hand to keep it from hitting the drink. "At least he didn't crap on our heads like a seagull."

Cole looked warily upwards at the skylarking Bogart. "Yet."

CHAPTER TWENTY-SEVEN

Parnell hunched over his desk, depressing Mallory with a display of documents bearing grim figures. Both of the City Hallers started as the door slammed open and Oakley strode into the room. Jancy, a redheaded secretary, was right behind him, outraged that he'd gotten past her. Without breaking his gaze at the two pols, Oakley pushed the door shut behind him, cutting her off. She kicked the door smartly from the outside. The pair looked at him with the eyes of men who have no idea what's happening but suspect they won't care for it. He said, "You guys still wish me all that luck with fetching your embezzler back?"

"Of course we do, Mr... Oakley," Parnell said in a soothing tone. "Do you need something from us?"

"A desk."

Mallory regarded him without expression or enthusiasm. "You need a desk."

Oakley nodded, completely serious. "Yep. Where I can sit and look through every file you have on Hunstetter."

"We provided you with..."

Oakley cut Parnell off with a raised palm. "Everything. Mortgages, family, friends, friends of family, families of friends, piss tests, pap smears, napkin doodles."

Oakley was sitting at the computer monitor on a hastily-vacated cubicle desk when Jancy slunk in the door, still showing signs of her redhead anger. With one hand she coldly dumped a stack of manila folders on the desk, with the other reluctantly proffered a cup of coffee. "They said bring you some."

134

Oakley nodded pleasantly and she defiantly said, "It's black." He smiled and reached for the cup and she said, "Re-heated instant."

Oakley looked at the coffee, then back at the petulant secretary. "Thanks, Red. I'll be needing it. Look, sorry I barged across your turf back there. I needed their attention and, well, they're jerks."

Jancy flashed him a freckly grin. "Tell me something I don't know."

Oakley regarded her a minute, sipping from the cup of lousy coffee. "Maybe it would work better the other way around."

Another secretary, severely dressed with salt and pepper hair cut to the point of being "butch", stepped into the door of the cubicle, where there were several coffee cups on the table, and a lot of butts in the ashtray in front of Jancy. Oakley and the redhead looked up from what was obviously a warm, sprawling conversation and were favored him with a vinegar look. "Jancy, you didn't..."

Oakley cut in politely but firmly. "Please tell Mr. Parnell that she's still assisting me in my ongoing investigation. Thank you."

Ms. Severe hesitated, stared bleakly at both of them, and retreated, not happy. Jancy rolled her chair back to peer down the corridor and make sure she was gone, then leaned forward in her gossip pose. "Someday somebody's going to bulldog her off the fender of a pickup. Probably her psycho girlfriend."

"I'd love to hear more about that some time," Oakley told her, smiling, "But I'm kind of pressed on this Hunstetter thing."

She leaned back and spread her arms. "I just don't know what more there is to tell you, honey. He was never exactly Mister Excitement."

"You were making his wife sound pretty exciting."

"Ellie Mae?" Jancy snorted. "I think he bought her her first pair of shoes and she wore 'em out from the inside. Now she's busy wearing out mattresses."

"Country girl, then? From around here?"

"Country to say the very least. She's got the only white neck in her whole family."

"Any idea where they live?"

"Dragknuckle Junction, I'd say," Then she thought of something. "Oh, except that retard brother of hers. Spends all his time playing video games with little boys out at that lot of his."

"Lot?"

"Lot of nothing now he doesn't have any more city hall connections to toss him tow jobs and impounds."

Oakley came down the worn marble steps of the Sulfur Springs courthouse three at a time and ran to his Fury--which was parked on the lawn--and spun out two divots as he left. Down the block past the drugstore, March pulled his damaged battlewagon away from the curb and followed him.

Where the town straggled out into bigger and bigger chunks of undefiled desert, the street becoming a highway with cracker slums on one side and prairie on the other, March got the picture on where Oakley was heading, and it made sense. The last outpost of low-rent urban sprawl was a big dilapidated garage with roll-up doors, a rusty link fence around a yard full of deteriorated junkers, and two faded signs: HARLAN'S TOW-N-STOW and,

MEAT LOCKERS, NOTARY PUBLIC. Putting it all together, March tightened up and banged a gear. With a throaty rumble, his powerwagon swooped out from behind the hay truck in whose wake it had been lucking and blasted up behind Oakley.

Who got a glimpse of the gunship from the Monclavo plaza fiasco and stomped on the superior power of the Fury, but not it time. March had gotten beside him just far enough to be able to cut harshly right, slam into his left rear fender, and drive him off the road. A brief but harrowing high speed duel continued out in the sagebrush, where the Fury had no advantage over the four-wheeling Denali. Oakley thought about his shotgun, but remembered the SUV had shown up as hard to kill back in the square, so he concentrated on fighting the wheel and trading bodyslams with the marauding March.

Skidding around on the yellow dust locally posing as Texas topsoil, Oakley was having some visibility problems, but hoped March might also lose some of his hard-pressing advantage. He braked and skidded, wheeled hard right and left, but couldn't find the purchase to shake the big Denali off his butt. He was considering a desperation move--cutting hard and braking into a drift that would bring wheels off the ground and risk rolling him if he hit anything bigger than a jackrabbit--when he plunged into a gulley. He fought the wheel hard as his tires crumbled the rim and nosed him over, but March was right in his blind spot, nerfing him into the cut, then pulling off to slide in a donut while Oakley's rig staggered, yawed, then rolled right over on its roof, wheels spinning up top, windows crammed down in the abandoned irrigation ditch, making the doors inoperable. March watched the Fury for a minute, covering it heavily with a matte black Swedish assault rifle. Assured there was no movement from that Santa Claus old fart that had been inside, he hit the gas and wheel in reverse, spinning around almost in place, and gunned it back towards the highway.

He wheeled back to the road in a geyser of gritty dust, spun onto hardtop and raced right up to the garage's link fence. He exited his SUV on the side away from building, scanning the two choppers and the shiny new Escalade parked in front of the Tow-N-Stow double doors. He'd run the plates on the Caddy on sight: recently stolen from the marina up on the reservoir. And those shot-out Hardly Drivinsons made it pretty clear who was in there. Just exactly the people he was looking for. He popped the rear of the Denali, slid out one of those menace-insinuating black cases his type seem drawn to, and walked up on a low knoll between the road and the garage, keeping a sharp eye on all the doors and windows.

Sliding into the shade of discouraged-looking scrub, he opened the case and started ritualistically slapping together the components of an extremely serious custom sniper rifle with ported suppressor on the business end, folding bipod, modified schuetzen-style curved stock at the back, and a lot of obsessively machined alloy in between, including a heavy-duty magazine with BAR background and indications that it was ready to feed in something in the .50 caliber range for semi/full automatic dispersal. Sighting in the 40x scope and adjusting for wind made him about as content as he ever got. He looked through the suspended crosshairs, faintly three-dimensional in the slight greenish tint of the Savorski lens elements, and prepared for quick shots at the door, all the front windows, and the strategic positions on the vehicles. Then he lay in wait.

CHAPTER TWENTY-EIGHT

The dead storage bay inside the Tow N Stow was dusty, dusky, and ripe with the odors of transmission fluid, strawdust, and ancient horse manure. It was lined with shelves of warped, unfinished wood heaped with junk ranging from parts for remotely conceivable automobiles to remnants of failed painting and drywall businesses, to collections of outmoded music and gaming devices; eight-track tapes lying amid X-box cartridges and Commodore joysticks. A dowdy Pacer had been carefully backed into the stall, and it sat there with its trunk lid yawning open. A set of golf clubs flew out from behind the hatch hood, then a shower of blankets, jumper cables, highway flares and other trunk trash.

Then the lid slammed down with a triumphant sound, revealing Bunny, Cole, the Bike Scum, and Hunstetter, all staring at a briefcase Cole was laying on the trunk lid. He looked at the locks and shot a glance at Hunstetter, who leaned on his short, awkward crutches, patted his pants, and shook a sheepish head. Flathead struck like a rattler, his switchblade flashing up and under the lock tabs. He twisted, the tabs flew off, and Cole opened the case to peer inside. They all stood silent, stunned by the rigid green rows and lascivious zeros in the case. Ahhhhhhhh! Cole reached out to touch the money, then stopped and slammed the case shut.

Turning to Bunny, he said, "Best you take it into hand, Bunnyhug. Know how it goes with me and money."

Bunny leaned to kiss his cheek, then took the case and hefted it, humming happily. The bikers' eyes, widened in awe, followed every move the case

140

made. She smiled at Hunstetter. "I don't think we've been giving you enough respect, Alvin."

Bogart recovered enough to give a long, low whistle and almost whispered, "That's a lot of scorpion belt buckles, all right."

"Let's all go sit down," Bunny said. "It's payday."

There was an instant crush towards the door of the bay, but Bogart stopped to wave Bunny ahead with a courtly flip of his hand and a slight bow.

In the dumpy office, elaborate video gaming devices the only objects in sight not covered with dust and in some way broken, Bunny sat primly at Harlan's desk, the case open in front of her, counting stacks of bills. Everyone else just gaped and waited. Finally she selected a stack of thousands and looked up into the row of expectant eyes on the ratty sofas along the other wall. "Okay, guys," she said briskly to the bikers. "We promised you a hundred thousand, but you came through really good and we did better than we thought. So here's a nice even half million. Spend it wisely, now. I'd stay out of the Chingazo until it's gone."

Bogart and Flathead were speechless, swiveling outraged gazes back and forth from her to each other. Their faces furrowed in anger, they started to speak, but Hunstetter cut in and stalled them out. "Very generous."

The saddletramps stared at him, completely nonplussed, their aggrieved protests suspended by his palpable lame-ness. "We didn't really set a figure on what I'd pay you to help me," he went on, "But I think a million would be pretty good pay for three day's work."

Now Cole and Bunny joined in the disbelieving stares. Cole broke the tableau by laughing out loud, and the bikers joined in. Bunny just smiled sadly at him, shaking her head. Now he stared around stunned. Light dawned on Marblehead. "No, no," he squeaked. "This is my... Do you know what I went through for this? I... You're *stealing* it from me!"

Cole pointed a pistol finger at him. "Where'd you get it, Hotshot?"

Hunstetter started to reply, then lapsed into a distraction so deep and gesticulating, Bunny was afraid he was going to fall off his crutches and succumb to some sort of fit. "You don't understand how it works," he finally managed to sputter. "Here, look, let me show you something."

He stumped over by Bunny on the stubby crutches and reached for the briefcase. His motion was so natural, she let him touch it. He snatched the case, spun awkwardly on his mini-crutches and plowed piecemeal towards the outside door. Everyone in the room was caught so off-guard by this move out of the timid accountant that he actually made it to the door before they reacted. But Cole took one gliding step and caught him at the door. Bunny was right behind him, incensed. She yelled, "You give that back right this minute, you little crook!"

Cole grabbed the case, but Hunstetter hung on doggedly, worrying it like a pit bull with a bone. All three stumbled out into daylight. Cole snatched the case away, but Hunstetter lunged for it and fell off his spindly perch on the crutches.

Suddenly, in mid-stumble, he spun around as if kicked by a pro punter, blood gushing from his shoulder. A second later a harsh report slammed into the walls behind them. In one fluid motion Cole drew, spun, fired, and pushed Bunny back inside. He jumped to stand inside the door, firing towards the knoll. His answer was a burst of automatic fire that blew big pieces out of the wall.

Cole pounced out the door, one hand pointing at the area on the knoll where he'd seen a tiny muzzle flash, and poured out covering fire. The other hand found the collar of Hunstetter's jacket and snatched him off the ground as he fell back through the door. The little CPA flew over Cole's supine body and crashed into the office while Cole kept firing, sighting over the toes of his boots until Bunny slammed the door shut.

Somebody had obviously reloaded, because a rattle of automatic fire raked the front of the garage. Windows blew inward, thumb-sized slugs came right through wall and blew slivers of plastic out of the game boxes, objects exploded and shattered, nobody in the office stood over six inches tall.

The fusillade ended, there was single shot, then it got quiet.

Bunny was examining the big, alarming, wound in Hunstetter's shoulder as he lay sobbing on the floor. Both bikers had produced nasty-looking firearms and peered out the window, sharing their theories. Cole lowered himself into Harlan's chair, ignoring the hole blown in the headrest, and placed the briefcase firmly behind him.

Having staunched the bloodflow, if not Hunstetter's whimpering, she looked up while tying a bandage improvised from some Mario Brothers T-shirts Bogie had found in a file cabinet. "I can see you haven't learned a thing about running right into the bullets to grab stuff up," she said in a forbidding tone.

Bogart, who'd seen where that sort of thing could lead, tried to head her off. "Aw, come on. He saved this wienie's life. He was heroic."

Bunny withered him with a glare. "And we know how heroes end up, don't we, now?"

"Why do *I* always get shot?" Hunstetter wailed from the floor. "I'm the only one not trying to."

"You got a rare knack for it," Cole told him. "Not a doubt about that."

Bunny dusted her hands and leaned back from her medical attentions. "Nicked a bone on this one, I think. But nothing really broken up in there."

"But it *hurts!*" Hunstetter bawled. "See my point?"

"Don't you get sassy, now," she said primly. "I'm just trying to stop you bleeding to death."

"I'm thinking that's your same old buddy out there," Cole mused. "Don't think he'd mind a bit if you bled to death and back again.

"Sounded like two different guns," Flathead said, and Bogart nodded agreement.

"Well, hell," Cole threw up his hands, "They got us surrounded."

On the grassy knoll, Oakley, bleeding from the bumps he took when his car flipped over, as well as the scratches from crawling out the broken windshield, stood looking at his feet. Or rather, right in front of his feet, at the sprawled body of the black-clad hitman whose name he didn't know, but couldn't see that it made any difference at that point, since March reclined over a sophisticated sniping rifle and a spray of cranial blood. He took a deep breath, regretting the various pops and pain-sparkles through his body as he did. Then squared off and

144

walked in towards the garage buildings. Where he figured he'd find his quarry.

CHAPTER TWENTY-NINE

The bikers wanted to get back to discussing money, but having a sniper on their case seemed to be a bigger priority, so they kept a close eye out the shattered front office window while trying not to present too tempting a target. Whoever it was hadn't opened up again, though, had he? Suddenly Bogart was on alert, nudging Flathead with his boot. "Hey, here's some dumb motherfucker right now. Rolling right up on us."

Flathead peered out the window and grunted in surprise. "Whoa, it's the geezer who cold-cocked that ninja dickhead with the frypan."

Cole stepped to the window and Bunny immediately left Hunstetter's side to sit by the briefcase. He watched Oakley striding in out of the sun and nodded admiringly. "Ballsy sunbitch."

Oakley strode purposefully out of the desert and in through the gate to stop twenty paces out from the door, standing flatfooted and awaiting acknowledgement.

Flathead scratched his burr head with the hand not occupied aiming his chunky Brazilian .45 right at Oakley's breadbasket. "What do we do about this fool?"

Cole called out to Oakley, keeping his own pistol on point. "What you selling, Lone Ranger?"

"I don't care whatever funny business you got going. I just want Hunstetter."

All eyes shot to the accountant, who frantically shook his head and motioned "No" with both hands, then grimaced in pain.

"He's shot up bad enough now," Cole announced in a loudspeaker voice.

146

"Not my doing."

Bogart had his whole head above the jagged bottom of the window by then, staring at this bold moron. "You a cop?"

"Far from it. Bounty hunter."

"They suck, too."

"I'll be right in," Oakley announced.

Everybody looked around, then at Cole, who shrugged, then called out. "Bring in them crutches, can you?

The big bounty-hunter's presence in the office did little to reduce the tension. Bunny guarded the money, glaring at anybody who ogled it. The bikers looked ready to shoot Oakley in solidarity with busted brothers, or just on general principles. Hunstetter sat on the floor, casting around for a savior. Cole was squared off at Oakley and frowning. "Now, see, we said we'd cut him loose. He paid us. Well, sort of."

Oakley nodded in understanding, but said, "I have to haul him in. Aside from that whole law thing, it's a matter of professional reputation."

"I got mine as well," Cole said stubbornly.

The standoff got silent then, and more than a little edgy. The bikers were tensed and thinking pointedly of their firearms, and Bunny was so apprehensive she didn't even have anything to say, when Cole suddenly brightened. "Hold on, here. He stole this money, right?"

There were nods around the room, Oakley starting to get the picture that this kid was a cutie, and had amazing hands, but wasn't exactly a brain scientist. "OK, then," Cole concluded, "He gotta pay for it. Stealing ain't right."

That one silenced everybody in the room and drew long, big-eyed stares. Cole took notice of this and shrugged again. "Completely different thing. He stole from people who trusted him. We steal from people who *don't* trust us, right? Look at their whole rig-up and what do you see? They *expect* to get stole from."

"So that makes it okay?" Oakley asked, hiding his smile.

"What can I say?" Cole asked academically. "It's *their* expectations."

Bunny regarded him with mixed affection and condescension. "Simply amazing."

Oakley just nodded to Cole and reached down to pull Hunstetter to his feet and slap the crutches into his hands. "So I can take this dickhead and walk?"

"Works for me."

"Thanks for being an upstanding citizen." Oakley turned to Hunstetter and said, "We'll wait out by the road. I've got a wrecker on the way."

"Wait," Bunny said quietly, and Oakley turned a gentlemanly expression towards her. "There's one other thing." She pulled a plastic liner out of the trashcan, dumped a fistful of money packages in it, and wrapped it tight. She searched in a drawer, found some rubber bands, snapped them around the bundle, and tossed it to Oakley. "That's a million dollars," she told him. "Take that, too."

An almost audible shock passed through the entire company. Bunny drew a lot of stares from men, but seldom of the current intensity. Cole was the first to find his voice. "Now Shoog, I don't know..."

"He seems honorable enough," she said. "He can tell them he recovered it when he caught Hunstetter."

148

Bogart and Flathead, now doubly enraged, went into a two-part harmony of disgust.

"Are you out of your fucking mind, woman?" Bogie yelled.

"Fuck that," Flatty bellowed, "A million fucking bucks to...

"What the fuck are you fucking thinking the fuck about fucking up?"

"...these assholes?   We only got a fucking half million!"

"Fuck!"

"Fuck!"

Ignoring the obscene duet, she told Cole, "I always wanted to be the sort of person who could donate a million bucks to a good cause."

What a gal! Oakley grinned as she continued. "We *did* shoot up their bank, Hon. Injured their policemen and all."

"Hey, that's the breaks of the game," he answered quickly. "You give that back, how many years before we're broke again and just have to do it all over?"

She stood and beckoned him close, stroked the side of his neck. "We shouldn't wait that long, should we? Don't want you getting rusty."

"You know me, Sugarpie. Rather bust out than rust out."

His acquiescence to her obviously insane scheme sent the Bike Boyz into another duet.

"Are you fucking serious???" Bogart screamed.

"You gotta know whose side you're on..." Flathead joined in.

"This guy works for the fucking *man*!"

"...you crazy broad!"

"You're just buying into the fucking *system*..."

Fucking do something with her, Haskins!"

"...don't you *see* that?"

"Before somebody else has to!"

Calmly, Bunny explained herself to Cole. "Look, getting a little money back will take a lot of heat off. And I think it'll motivate Mister Bounty Hunter here..."

"Name's Oakley, Ma'am."

Bunny nodded at the introduction. "Hello, Oakley. I'm Bunny, that's Cole. And those two over there are disgruntled ex-employees. I was saying you might be motivated to sort of cut us a little slack."

The Bikers were on their feet at that, guns in their waistbands. They faced the others defiantly. Hunstetter implored them with a look, glanced sideways at Cole and Oakley. Who stepped in front of him, his arms hanging loose. Open for business.

Cole also adopted a trouble-ready stance and no-shit look. The Bikers fumed, boiling inside, but stood down and walked to the door sizzling with frustration. At the door, Flathead turned and pointed a shaking finger at Cole, but couldn't find words sufficient to express his disgust. Bogart's face was a mask of betrayed hurt. "You people are *sick.* You should be, like, barred from the whole robbery profession."

Flathead turned on his heel for a dramatic stomp-out, but suddenly remembered the shooter outside and peered cautiously around the doorjamb.

"Don't worry," Oakley said from behind him. "Nobody out there any more."

The bikers stomped out in a huff, the very blat and vroom of their choppers taking on their disaffected attitude as they roared to life and blasted away.

Cole shot Oakley a look of guarded professional assessment. "So you took care of that machine gun guy?"

Oakley produced a black Ballistic wallet from his coat pocket and handed it over. "The late Overton March. The guy who's been shooting you, Hunstetter."

"So you up and killed him?"

"That last shot you heard after he nailed Alvin, here."

"Well, thank you very much. Good man. You gonna keep the money, aren't you?" Cole fanned the wallet, offering it to him.

"No thanks. I don't kill people for money. I think maybe Mr. March did, though. If you want to bring people in, you don't use a target rifle with a high power scope."

Cole nodded and pocketed the cash. Bunny stepped over, browsing the credit cards. She pulled out a foil-wrapped condom and rolled her eyes.

Hunstetter had been taking it all in, and was completely horrified. "My *God!* He was going to *kill* me? Can he collect the bounty if I'm dead?"

"Don't give me any ideas," Oakley told him.

Bunny directed some attention to the bounty hunter, on her own discovery. "So you just, what, walked up behind that man and shot him dead?"

"Kind of looked like he was murdering people. One of whom..." he pointed a proprietary finger at Hunstetter, "Is my property. At least until duly redeemed."

"Plugged him in the back?"

"Seemed best at the time."

"So you didn't consider just shooting him in the hand or anything?" Bunny asked with some interest. "Letting him draw first?"

"I'm a pro, Ma'am. No style points. That stuff's just for the movies."

"You hear that, Cole? This man is a professional. I want you to listen."

Incredulous, Cole protested, "I ain't quite amateur league night myself. A body wants to try to outdraw my ass, I'll put up money."

"You stop that, Cole. We *got* money. Now what we gotta get is out of here."

"That would be my advice," Oakley nodded. He buttoned his coat and tucked the bundle of money inside.

Hunstetter stared at him apprehensively. "Can I ask a question, here? How do you keep finding me? How did that guy keep finding me and shooting me?"

Oakley reached into Hunstetter's pocket, extracted his wallet and showed him the transmitting device.

"*Another* one? Do I need to get an underground radio station license or something? Sell commercial time?"

Oakley slid Parnell's magnetic bug out of his own pocket and showed it to them, then dropped it back in. "That one's a little embarrassing, actually. It was a lot more obvious once he turned my car upside down for me."

"So," Hunstetter asked timorously, "Is anybody else going to show up with guns and bad manners?"

152

CHAPTER THIRTY

On a lone desert highway, wind in their hair, Bogart and Flathead buzzed through the warm night side by side. "I told you to go for a percentage," Bogart reminded Flathead again. "But no, you have to give 'em a flat fee."

"Plus expenses. Which we forgot to itemize, by the way. We didn't know how sweet the deal was, okay?"

"The smart money always goes for the points, not pay."

"Points?! Where are you getting this shit, Sprockethead? And what the fuck is 'smart money'? It's like saying 'smart pussy'. It lays there and you grab it. No smarts about it. Shit!"

"That attitude is why we're always broke," Bogart reproved. "Hey! Look up ahead."

Beyond a slight rise in the road, they could see a sort of local Northern Lights display, the dusty sky pulsing in faint red and blue glow. Not unaccustomed to that sort of light display, the cyclists split, heading into the cover of brush on both sides of the road. Immediately two police cars zoomed by, running fast with light bars strobing but no sirens. As the cops disappeared in the direction of the tow yard, the two putted into the middle of the road, looking at the dwindling light show, then at each other. Both nodded and they spun their wheels around to head back for a look-see.

In the Tow-N-Stow office, Oakley had Hunstetter in a firm grip, his other hand on the knob of the riddled front door.   "Well, thanks for everything. Good luck, kids."

"Yeah, we'll have to do this next year," Cole drawled. "You can give us a million, make it a yearly thing."

"I'll mark it on my calendar." He opened the door and glanced through, just as the two cruisers skid up to the fence, pulsing colors.   Cole was instantly up, gun in hand and kicking the door shut. He glared at Oakley, who gave him a bored look and pushed Hunstetter down onto the couch.

"Not my doing," he said firmly. "Your misfortune and none of my own."

Cole's ears pricked up at a series of barely intelligible rumbles and commands sounded outside. Finally somebody with know-how got the loudhailer in hand and they could all make out: "Everybody inside! Throw your guns out the window and come out one at a time with your hands in the air."

Oakley rolled his eyes, shook his shaggy head wearily, and pulled out his credentials. He opened the door and stepped outside, holding his ID wallet above his head. "Hey boys. I'm a licensed..."

A pepper of small-arms fire cut his introduction short. He dived back into the door, rolling on the floor and staring back outside with a highly pissed-off expression. "There's a whole lot of cops plain give me a case of the red-ass."

While the four young cops from the responding cars rehashed their shooting and hit vigilant poses, a third car arrived and pulled softly in beside them to create a long cordon outside the lot fence. Put on their mettle by the new arrival, the officers on the scene crouched behind their cars, pointing sidearms

154

in two-handed Academy grips. A rather callow patrolman stuck his head out the window and asked, "Was that them we heard shooting?"

"Naw," a freckly ex-jock with six months on the job replied, "That was us. But they've got assault rifles and shit."

The new arrival stared at the garage, nodding in excitement. "Coooool!"

Oakley moved towards the door again, causing Bunny to slip behind the desk and Hunstetter to roll hurriedly onto the floor and clasp his hands behind his head. "Let's see if those morons have got any adult supervision yet."

He carefully pushed the door open, waited while not drawing any immediate fire. Still behind the jamb he started to call out, but Hunstetter beat him to it. "*Help!*" he wailed, "These maniacs are holding me captive. Get me out of here!"

Oakley slammed the door and glared at him, hands on hips. Hunstetter shrugged, "I don't see any reason to speed this process up any."

Out in the police cordon, which was gradually enlarging, the callow cop was practically hugging himself in glee. "Oh, mama. Looks like we got a hostage situation on our hands."

"*Way* cool!" his freckled colleague hooted. An older officer, sitting on the hood of his unit sipping coffee from a thermos, scowled. "Christ. You know that's gonna bring the TV vans out here like bass hitting chum."

"Outstanding!" the callow newbie exclaimed. "Bet I get an interview with Cathy Crandell on Channel Five! She is soooo hot."

"Ya freaking rookie. It means we'll be here all night. Did you call the Captain?"

The rookie looked away while his sallow-faced buddy told him, "Uh, yeah, sure we did. Think we're stupid or something?"

The veteran sighed. "Go call him, you bimbo."

By the time Captain Garvey pulled up and exited his car, there were a half-dozen other cars at the scene, and a dozen milling policemen waiting for the action. He surveyed the deployment, the motioned to the knoll. "I expect a couple of you got deer rifles in your cars like you're not supposed to?"

Two of his men grinned sheepishly and pulled scoped hunting rifles out of their trunks. "Get up on that rise there, you two." He pointed, but held their eyes before letting them go. "Might have to do some sniping. Watch the windows and the back. Be sensible, you hear?"

The riflemen moved off towards the higher ground, flashlights bobbing. Garvey looked around the barricade and picked up a bullhorn off a trunk lid. He fingered the trigger, getting attention with an amplified click or two, then said, "This is Captain Garvey. We've got all the time in the world to sort this out. Let's get through it without any more shooting."

The door immediately flew open and Cole, sheltered behind the doorjamb, thrust his arm out and kicked off six shots so fast they sounded like automatic fire. Six of the squad car lights exploded as men leaped for cover. The other lights were quickly extinguished

156

Cole closed the door and reloaded, telling Bunny and Oakley, "The red ones are worth five and the blue ones are ten. I don't know why. Just the rules of the game."

"That'll sure make them easier to talk to," Oakley said, more amused than irritated. "Look, things are tightening up. And they'll keep getting tighter with your nuts in the middle. It's time to talk."

"Time like this," Cole told him, "I got but one thing I care to say." He leaned back on his boot heels, cupped his hands around his mouth and hollered, "Come and get me, coppers!"

Oakley eyed him a minute, then offered, "Why not let me talk to them for you? What the hell?"

"God knows I've tried to talk sense for him," Bunny sniffed. "You can see for yourself how far it got me."

"It's just going to get worse."

Bunny nodded unhappily at that, looking around the office in search of escape routes or bright ideas. Just then they heard one of the hunters on the rise call urgently to Garvey, "Captain! You'd better get up here, take a look at this."

Oakley watched a dozen MagLite beams ascending the knoll and sighed. He turned to Cole, "Guess they found Mr. March."

"I'd much prefer Miss September, myself."

"You best not be talking that way..." Bunny began, but of all things, the phone rang.

Cole, as if expecting a call, stepped over and answered it. "How do? I demand a stretch limousine--make it a Hummer--to take us to the airport. And a jumbo jet waiting for us. One of them big ones with cocktail lounges upstairs. Case a longneck Buds and a can of Red Man."

Fourteen miles away, a door bearing the name DUNEBUSTERS CHOP AND SHOP hung off its hinges, no longer protecting a floor cluttered with Baja bugs, racing bikes, and sand rails. Bogart was in his element, eagerly sparking an arc welder, as Flathead spoke into the phone. "Demand in one hand, shit in the other, see which fills up first."

Cole heard the man out, regarded the phone a moment, then cupped the receiver to his chest and looked at Bunny. "Yo, Scooterpie."

"Is that some sort of negotiator?" Bunny asked pointedly, already figuring out how to get the phone away from her bumptious boyfriend.

"Well, sort of a different type negotiation. How much money you still feel like giving away today?"

CHAPTER THIRTY-ONE

The cops at the embattled line went alert as the door of the Tow-N-Stow office opened with visible movement inside. A white cloth waved through the crack, billowing long enough to draw spotlights and let everybody get used to it and calm down. Then Oakley's voice came; loud enough be heard, but low enough to carry unhurried authority. "Hey, listen, out there. I have the hostage. He's safe. I just want to come out and bring him with me. But I don't want any rough stuff or indignities. I'm a professional."

Hoisting the bullhorn, Garvey asked, "Professional what?"

"Skip tracer. Name's Oakley. I've got Hunstetter here and am bringing him in for the bail."

Garvey pondered that a moment, then keyed the loudspeaker down again, "Working for Battles?"

"You got it."

There was another pause before Garvey came back, "I thought they had some other guy on this. You'd better let me run some checks. Just keep calm."

And no reason not to, because there was nothing else to do. So they all waited, some more calmly than others. Garvey was standing on one foot, prying a goathead burr out of the seam on the back of his other boot when his freckle-faced patrolman approached him diffidently, showing him a length of fax paper. "Cap, I think you'd better look at this."

Without looking up from his boot, Garvey said, "Are you looking at it?"

Taken aback, Freckles mumbled, "Well, yeah. Course I am."

"So tell me about it."

Switching to Official Cop Info Voice, the younger man held the fax in a headlight beam and squinted into the glare. "It's a make on the other two in there with Hunstetter and this bounty guy. They're both wanted."

"You mean that shitwad who shot my lights off committed crimes?"

"Armed robbery, bank robbery, assault deadly weapon, vehicular assault, attempted murder, grand theft..."

"Wait a minute. They do that bank job down in Chisolm? Shot the security guard?"

"That'd be them. Cole Haskins and Beatrice Beaumont, aka 'Bunny'."

Garvey set his foot down and reached. "Lemme see that."

He took the printout and scanned it thoughtfully under the bluish gleam of his MagLite. "Beautiful woman. Couple of good-looking, likely kids. What gets into 'em these days?"

"Drugs," his protégé answered immediately. "That rap hop music."

Garvey lowered the printout and stared at the rundown building, taking in its isolation, its shot-up door and windows, its six sagging garage doors. He turned and surveyed his manpower, which looked like about every man on the force by now. "So all we got here is a couple of dangerous armed felons known to put cops in intensive care, a crooked politician, a bounty hunter and a dead hitman?"

"Plus maybe a couple million bucks."

Garvey turned away wearily, heading for his glove compartment where he seemed to recall he'd stashed a pint of sippin' bourbon. "Best get on the horn, get some help down here."

"I'll call county, Captain."

"Just this county?"

Time wasn't passing any faster or more carefree inside the embattled office. The four inhabitants' postures all reflected a long tedious evening and small hopes it would improve. Hunstetter was torn between being thoroughly sick of the place and decidedly unwilling to leave it and get back to the tender mercies of Texas incarceration. His brief sample of life behind bars had persuaded him it was less than an idyll and greatly to be avoided. Not that he'd figured out a way to avoid it. But the night was still young.

Bunny peeped out the front window for the umpteenth time and got the same information as the last dozen times. "They just keep sending more cops."

"Would sending some coffee be too much to ask?" Cole asked rhetorically. "Spare us a coupla jelly donuts?"

"They just might resent you shooting up their light equipment," Oakley mildly reminded him from the straight chair he leaned by the door to monitor and detain Hunstetter, should the issue arise.

Slumped on the couch, gripping his dwarf crutches, Hunstetter's continued his ceaseless mental machinations, aimed at trying to understand and subvert his situation. And they had just raised a question in his mind. "When he said they, 'had some other guy', he meant March, right?"

"I'd think so," Oakley said, thought it over a second. "That's kinda interesting, all right."

"So he didn't come from that black guy, he came from the city. Which means Parnell or Mallory. Or both. This whole thing was their baby. Their cash cow."

"Dirty politicians?" Bunny asked in feigned shock.

"Sendin' out killers to rip off city money is fairly dirty, Lambchop."

"Those creeps are old-timers. They damn near built city hall around Mallory."

Oakley was worrying it around, but couldn't get a handle on it. He shook his head at the prospect, "Doesn't add up. Their chances of finding you weren't that good. You shook that moron they put on your tail. They'd have been better off just waiting for me to bring you back."

"And why hire a jerk like that?" Bunny wondered. "No surprise he tried to steal the money for himself."

"Exactly. Besides, he was shooting to kill."

"Could we not dwell on that?" Hunstetter pleaded from the couch.

"Well, you don't shoot into the center body mass from that range without cause of death being a distinct possibility."

Cole nodded. "Cleverly falling on your ass is the only thing saved you."

"Actually none of it makes any sense at all." Oakley was getting intrigued. "It's almost like they planned on getting ripped off."

"Maybe the bondsman did send that March after you," Bunny tossed out. "He could have planted that bug on your car."

"No. I trust Battles all the way. Known him and worked with him for years. We have the same ethic."

Cole stared. "How can that be? He a spade or ain't he?"

"He said 'Ethic', Punkin. Not 'ethnic'."

"Anyway," Oakley went on, "You already failed to appear. If you're dead, the bail's forfeited and Battles is out money."

162

"That's how they work it?" Bunny asked.

"Of course. If you don't show up, they keep the bond money. That's the whole principle of bail."

Sooooo....." Bunny drew it out, pursing her lips. "If they kill Hunstetter, the city gets to keep six million dollars?"

There was a silence as everybody stared at Bunny, then each other. Hunstetter sat up, mouth falling open, as Oakley chuckled. "When you explain it like that, Lady, it kinda falls into place."

Cole glowed with reflected pride. "Sharp as a tack, that girl. Had a year of college."

"Junior college," Bunny demurred.

"Well, you sure tuned the picture in, I'm thinking."

Hunstetter was overcoming an attack of speechless outrage, but managed to squeak, "My God. Those...those *dicksuckers!*"

"Got to admire their thinking, though," Cole mused. "Wouldn't occur to most folks."

"Yes, it's ingenious," Hunstetter said bitterly. "What it is, it's ironic. That lousy Mallory."

Their mutual epiphany on the ways of Sulfur Springs' leadership was broken off by Captain Garvey on the bullhorn. "Oakley! Still awake in there, big fellah? Everybody okay?"

Oakley stood up and looked around the group. "We ought to have a plan here, don't you think?"

Garvey studied the Tow-N-Stow as the county medical van slipped in behind him, two paramedics hopping out the back door. They asked a Sergeant where the injured parties were, but Garvey just pointed towards the garage and held up the bullhorn to shut everybody up. All eyes turned to the office as

163

his voice reverberated in the night air. "Okay, the ambulance is here. Everybody's got the word to stay cool and collected. Why don't you bring our boy out now?"

From inside, Garvey called, "I'm coming out unarmed, carrying Hunstetter because he's shot. My credentials will be hanging from his feet. I'm the good guy, okay?"

In the bullhorn voice, Garvey replied, "Until we clear you, we'll have to assume..."

But Garvey trumped his amplification. "Did I mention I've got the money?"

CHAPTER THIRTY-TWO

Oakley sat on the sill of the rear door of the aid van, swabbing idly at his cuts from the roll-over and talking to Garvey. Behind him, the paramedics did preliminary treatment on Hunstetter's various gunshot souvenirs. They wanted to dash him to the county hospital, but Garvey wanted the unit there for awhile longer. He had a feeling there were going to be more casualties before this thing sorted itself out. Hunstetter himself, handcuffed to a folding gurney, was in no great hurry to depart. Garvey got off his radio and sized Oakley up again. "I sure hope we treated you gently enough to suit your tender sensibilities."

"And I appreciate it. After awhile you get sick of getting frisked on the ground for just doing your job."

"So what job, exactly, you doing here?"

"Trailing Hunstetter. Well, actually I was trailing another bounty hunter. Big guy, workout addict. Definitely dirty."

"We had a look at him. Looks like he's some sort of professional hitman."

"No kidding? Anyway, I took the money, collared Hunstetter, disarmed those crazies inside. But I'd bet they've re-armed themselves by now."

Garvey hesitated for a respectable length of time, then said, "Now about that money..."

Oakley pulled the trash bag bundle out of his jacket and tore it open, flashing a huge wad of G-notes. "Do I get a receipt?"

"Shit fire and save matches!" Garvey exclaimed. "That all of it?"

Oakley shrugged. "This looks like about a million from here. How much went missing?"

165

Garvey was very conscious of the huge amount of money locked in his trunk as he surveyed the scene of the siege. The air was just starting to lighten up with the rosy fingers of false dawn and he was unexpectedly pleased to be standing in that dramatic scene shift with the money in hand, the hostage/fugitive in cuffs, and all the goodun's extracted from the storage site. Of course there was still the matter of two armed and dangerous criminals to be flushed out and variously processed, but he figured he had them pretty well treed.

Or not. The golden silence of desert daybreak disintegrated as two snarling, hopped-up Chenowth sand rails--functional cages on fat tires driven by tweaked motors for the purpose of staving off boredom by blasting around desert environments--raced in from out of the sunrise, spitting sand from their fat paddle tires and popping their front wheels off the ground tauntingly. The rails blasted between police vehicles, scattering startled cops, bashed open both of the twin gates in the lot's fence, and roared up to the Tow-N-Stow. One of the garage doors rolled up and they zipped inside. The door slammed down with a very final rattle and quiet returned, accompanied by scattered confusion and consternation.

Garvey had no idea what was going on, but was livid at the surprise incursion. "What the hell kind of security we got here anyway, you clowns?"

"You don't normally expect people to break *in* to a hostage siege situation like this, Cap," a husky Sergeant said, but he was obviously embarrassed at this development.

"Godalldammit!" Garvey spat, dragging off his white department Resistol and slapping the brim against his thigh in frustration. "Probably brought 'em more food and ammo."

The freckled patrolman had another thought on that. "Or maybe it's so they can..."

Suddenly the rails exited the building with a vengeance, tearing the garage door right out of its frame in brute reverse acceleration. They spun like dancers in twin cyclones of dust, then blitzed straight out through the line of stunned law enforcement personnel.

"...escape or something," the young cop finished as the rails bumped out over the desert, launched high into the air by moguls, spewing rooster tails of dust glowing gold in the sunrise. They were a hundred yards out before a few cops opened belated fire.

"Don't bother shooting the tires," Garvey bullhorned. "They're solid Desert Dawgs for running over bob wire. And they got no radiators. Just get the hell after 'em!"

Cops scrambled for their cars and patched out in chase. Three younger officers were dismayed when a Sergeant waylaid their rush to join in a coveted open country chase, bullying them into a search of the Tow-N-Stow premises. As the police fleet thundered off into the dust, Garvey turned the bullhorn all the way up and yelled, "Head 'em over towards the bluff."

In the suddenly lonely area in front of the tow lot gates, Oakley leaned back against the van's door frame, watching the police force race away in hot pursuit. He turned thoughtfully to Hunstetter; crippled, cuffed, and regarded glumly by a patrolman detailed to miss the automotive steeplechase over the flats in order to guard a geeky fuckup who was obviously totally helpless.

"You know something?" he murmured pensively. "I don't much cotton to having a killer sicced on me."

"Actually," Hunstetter pointed out, "He was sicced on me."

He paused, shuddered, "I didn't cotton to it, either."

"You want a little free professional advice?"

"Why?" Hunstetter pointedly looked down at the swathes of bandages on his legs and shoulder, rattled his handcuff against the steel tubes of the gurney. "Don't I look like I'm doing well enough on my own?"

"When you cross certain moral lines, things get blurred. In my opinion, very few cross back over. A man who embezzles from folks who trust him, no telling what he might do: stickups, even blackmail or extortion."

"You're just trying to cheer me up."

"I'm suggesting you think it over. They're all just opportunity crimes, each in its own way."

Hunstetter gave him a long searching look, then fumbled under his dressings and sling to pull out a comb and pass it through his sideburns.

"Take a good long look at what opportunities present to you here," Oakley pressed on. "And your motive."

Hunstetter blinked at him and he leaned over to tap twice on his bandaged chest with his forefinger. "Might consider drawing on your recent experiences. 'Nough said."

The sand rails were definitely faster and more agile in their natural desert habitat, but the cop cruisers had the advantage of numbers and had spread wide to harry them across the scrub and dust. It shaped up into a merry chase: Baja 1000 meets Dukes of Sand Hazard. Sand rails and squad cars left the ground from time to time: the rails handled the landings better. From a higher vantage, the chase took on a hauntingly familiar appearance: a phalanx of lawmen hounding the speeding rails out along a narrow outcropping that dropped off dramatically on three sides. Ten yards from the brink of a steep cliff, the rails skidded to a stop and sat still, throbbing with potential flight.

The dust settled and the pursuers closed cautiously in on the quarry. The cops, tense and apprehensive, watched the two rails chugging around, fretting back and forth at the precipice. Suddenly one rail jolted forward, sprung up on its fat rear tires and wheelied towards the drop-off. The cops cried out almost in unison as the racer plunged over the edge and cartwheeled off into space. They heard the sound of it bouncing on boulders and trees below, then the whoosh of the fuel igniting, followed by a gout of black smoke.

Garvey, pulling up at the tail end of the posse, dropped his radio microphone and slowly exited his car, staring at the angry column of smoke, hearing the crackle of brushfire below the rim. "Oh my God!" was torn out of him. "That beautiful girl."

The freckled cop, who'd been in his car during the short chase, stepped up beside him and touched his shoulder gently. "Maybe she's in the other buggy Captain. There's a chance."

Garvey stood shaking his head at the senselessness of it all. "Those idiots are in the hands of the Lord now."

Almost a mile to the north, on top of a stumpy mesa, it became more clear whose hands the events were in, and they were far from God-like. Flathead and Bogart were lying prone on the rim of the mesa, their choppers leaning at rest far enough back to be unseen. Below them, the cop armada was slowly closing in on the surviving sandrail while smoke billowed up from the other to be teased east by the morning breeze.

"Oh man," Flathead chided in disgust, "You just had to do a Thelma, didn't you?"

He spit aside and scowled at Bogie, who raised his remote control console and fiddled with the control, dowsing around with the telescope antenna. "No, wait. Wait... Aw, I thought I had a wheel spinning there. Fuck it, it's broke."

"You break *everything*, you fuckup!" Flathead bitched. "You touch it, zap, it's broke. No warranty, no chaser. Fucking broke."

"Oh yeah, bigshot? You don't wanna play Louise, how you going to play it?"

Flathead nodded at him grimly, then hefted his own remote and grimly stated, "Like those dumb bitches should've done in the movie."

Below, the remaining rail abruptly jounced to life. It spun a donut, skidded and sideslipped, then charged right at the constricting circle of The Law. Blasting between two patrol cars, badly mauling both of them, the rail immediately drew very heavy fire. Though at that point it had become apparent that the "drivers" of the rail were a rather odd couple: an inflatable love doll and a paper mâché *piñata* in the shape of Spiderman.

The rail didn't do that shabby a job of broken field running, plunging through the larger cars while

170

taking a massive barrage of pistol, rifle, and shotgun fire. But it didn't really have a chance. Bullets pierced the beer keg over the cockpit, spilling all its gasoline out. Essential electrical parts were scoured off the engine block by the harsh hail of lead. A shotgun salvo eviscerated Spidey, spilling a cascade of hard candy out into the dirt. The spunky little jitterbug coughed, sputtered, and lurched to a stop. The drizzle of fuel from the keg ignited, splashing a red roar of high-octane flame around the rail and infecting the sagebrush with a dozen smaller fires.

Cops, so often more attracted to spectacular violence than caution, crept closer to the raging heat and noxious smoke from the flaming tires, but many jumped away when the heat exploded the sex doll, splattering them with shreds of polyester wig, cheap lingerie, and flesh-colored plastic. The freckled cop jumped at the explosion, then again when a big hunk of hot vinyl hit the front of his uniform blouse. He picked it off and examined it, realizing he'd been impacted by the love doll's vagina ringed with acrylic pubies. Inspired, he held it to his mouth, clowning around with his tongue inside the former mannequin's privates. Ringing it with his fingers, he blew into the cavity, managing to inflate it like a balloon. He showed his partner the results, then slammed it into his other hand, loudly popping it. At the sharp report of the synthetic nooky rupturing, a dozen guns snapped around to point at this new threat. Shaking, he held up his hands defensively, dropping the offending genital. Garvey glowered at him, then stalked off towards his car while fire trucks were summoned to cope with the rapidly spreading brushfire.

Atop the mesa, the bikers slithered back from the rim, stood up and headed for their bikes. Bogart, game over, tossed his RC control over his shoulder. Flathead alertly lunged to catch it before it smashed on the bare caprock.

"I can still use that, you dumb shit!" he groused. "Why do you have to break everything? It's like a disease."

"Oh, excuse me, Louise. I didn't know you were planning a sequel."

"Not the point. It's expensive equipment. Shit, what's your main malfunction, you numbnuts?"

"All that gear you hog just slows you down."

"Slows *me* down? You serious or just trying to get bitch-slapped?"

"I said slooooow." Bogie dragged his hand in front of him as if the air was molasses. "Meaning I'll be inside having a beer by the time you drag your shit-for-wheels up to the Soft Touch."

"In your fuggin' dreams, fagbait."

Both cycle tramps dashed to jump astraddle and haul their raunchy asses off the mesa, hazardously jockeying for position. They might be newly minted millionaires, but they weren't about to slack off on the rituals and protocols of their tribe.

CHAPTER THIRTY-THREE

Dark as the inside of a black cat at midnight, basically. And just as cramped.

But then there was a fetching giggle and a few muffled bumps.

Cole Haskins' voice echoed in the compacted darkness, "Ouch, Lollypop."

A blue LED flashlight winked on, casting feeble, unearthly light on his face and Bunny's, about two inches away. Whatever stray photons got by them just revealed how close and stuffy it was, crammed into the trunk of the rumpled old Cougar. Very little excess elbow room, and barely enough legroom, headroom, and buttroom, for that matter.

"It's just so tight in here," Bunny complained right into Cole's ear.

"If we'da got in that Chrysler or some big ol' hog like that, they might have just peeked in on us, Sunbun. And notice the nice padded carpet," Cole replied with his tongue practically in her ear. "Sides, there's no such thing as 'too tight' in guy talk."

She chuckled and did more squirming against him. "How much longer should we stay in here?"

"Just long enough, Honeymunch. Jam up and jelly tight, like they say."

"Long enough for what? We're like anchovies in here."

"Well, long enough for this, for one."

Bunny sighed pleasantly, her lashes fluttering down like butterflies going to rest. "Um, you do the sweetest things sometimes.'

"Just settle down easy and enjoy the company, lover mine. Look me right in the eyes."

"It's not like I can look much of anywhere else, Cole."

"Good."

Whatever he was doing down there in the unlit spots, it coaxed some sweet sounds out of Bunny. The light flicked out at some point, but the murmurs continued.

Bunny and Cole slipped cautiously out of the Tow-N-Stow building, into a soft, quiet night. Moonless country dark, but after spending a day in the Cougar boot, it looked like the Milky Way to them. The cracker clapboard of the garage was still garlanded with yellow police tape but unguarded. They'd heard Harlan come and go, in the company of police officers who started out sympathetic to the plight of a businessman whose office and goods got bullet-hosed for no reason, but by the time they left were obviously ready to slap him silly.

And it wasn't actually completely unguarded. Harlan had wired the fence shut and dropped his two junkyard Rottweilers in the yard to keep prowlers from taking advantage of the demolished garage door and Swiss cheese office. As soon as they stepped out of the garage both dogs sprinted up to them and took up positions of challenge, growling territoriality and salivating menace. Cole's gun was out in a blur, but Bunny socked his shoulder for him. "Oh, fine. Shooting down defenseless pups, now, are we? You're getting a one-track mind any more. Narrow gauge at that."

"Now these mutts ain't exactly what I'd call frisky puppy-dogs," he replied, looking the alpha Rott right in the eye over a hand-filed front sight. "More like a matched set of hit monsters."

174

"Don't be such a baby." She bent at the waist, extending her hands, palms out. "Heya, boys."

She walked slowly towards the dogs; both snarled forbiddingly. Behind her, Cole extended his arm to take a dead bead. But when she moved her hand within slashing and gnashing distance, the Rotts seemed to confer, then sniffed it, wavering. She reached out underhand, scratching beneath the jaw of the bigger one. The other crowded in for more and she joyously rubbed both of them down as they frolicked under her. "Oh, you're not so tough, you guys. Just a bunch of big, sweet doggies, aren'tcha? Oh, yeah, you like that. Don't worry, the bad old cowpoke won't shoot you."

She turned to Cole, who whipped the gun behind his back and smiled disarmingly. She stood with the dogs licking her hands and rubbing up against her legs. "Well, Deadeye, shall we blow this popstand? Or what?"

They walked down the street, loose and warm, holding hands like schoolkids, the briefcase dangling from Bunny's other hand like a three million dollar lunchbox. It wasn't the sunniest side of Sulfur Springs by any means, and what little activity there was appeared thwarted or sinister. Bunny felt like skipping on the warped sidewalk, flanked by the romping Rottweilers.

They passed a very ostensible drug runner, leaning with studied casualness on the hood of an extremely flash Pontiac Grand Am with a functional hood scoop and scavenger pipes. He eyed Cole briefly, ogled Bunny surreptitiously, and regarded the dogs with unfeigned wariness. They stopped in front of him and didn't look like trade, so he had to say

175

something. "Fine pooches, you got there, cousins."

"Fine wheels you got there, neighbor," Cole replied.

The dealer--one of those stringy Arky types with lank black hair and skin so white it looked blue at his throat and wrists--and the Rotts examined each other with mutual suspicion while Cole gave the car a more serious once-over. "Got it on sale?"

"For sale, is what I'm all about." He gestured expansively to include his person, car, neighborhood, entire world full of stuff he could get his hands on if the price were right. "Anything moves on out if the price works."

Cole stood up from squatting to examine the suspension and pulled a fist full of thousands out of his jeans pocket. "That look like it works? And I'll throw in the mutts."

Bunny shot him a sharp look and stepped up to scan the dealer for defects. He had a multi-generational heritage of macho, bitch-slapping disdain for women, but something in his gut told him this was one skirt around with whom one did not fuck. "Wait a minute. You know how to take care of these guys? They've been really exploited and need a good home."

"Lady," the Arky said, for possibly the first time in his life, "I got the perfect place for them. And all they can eat."

Bunny remained dubious, but nodded. "Well... okay, then."

He tossed the keys and Cole snatched them out of the air, stepped around to the driver door and slipped in. The dealer took a good look at Bunny getting in the passenger side, and gently closed her door for her, another first. The car fired up and ran the lower ranges of its glasspacked rumble. She

176

leaned out the window, fussing with the bounding dogs. She waved goodbye to them as Cole nudged the muscle car out from the curb, checked his rear view mirror, then turned his wide-eyed gaze towards a rather splendid future approached by wide-open road. "Bye, guys. Be good, now, hear?"

The dealer waved to her, stuffed the big wad of cash into the pocket in front of his hoodie, and examined the dogs, who sat with their heads cocked, looking to him for further developments and direction. "You can start by eating anybody comes trying to take me off."

CHAPTER THIRTY-FOUR

Parnell sat directly across the usual battle-scarred table from Hunstetter, Mallory to one side in a folding chair the guards had shoved into the cramped attorney conference room. He slumped dejectedly in his ill-fitting county issue denim coveralls. Only jailbird I ever saw who looks better dressed in those overalls than his street clothes, Parnell was thinking. He leaned back from the table and gave Mallory a knowing glance.

Mallory was gentle and commiserating to a fault, a disillusioned uncle trying to make the best of an unfortunate cock-up not of his making. "Look, Al. The more you co-operate the better off you're going to be." He gave Parnell a nakedly contrived questioning look and got back an equally road-company acquiescent nod. "And maybe we can sweeten it up for you some."

Hunstetter came to some inner finality that showed on his face. He looked up and scanned them both with a hard, dry coldness that wasn't in his usual repertoire. Both were suddenly aware that this wasn't the man they knew, who they thought they had. He pulled out his comb and raked his sideburns, giving them a downright arrogant look. And said, "You want to cut a deal, punks, I'll need a lot more taste than that."

Parnell stared at him in unfeigned amazement, but Mallory smiled: things might get more interesting. He gestured around, taking in the institutional cell, the barred windows, the whole regrettable contretemps. "Aren't you the one who needs a deal?"

Hunstetter ignored him, fixing Parnell with a blunt gaze. "Gimme a smoke."

His hand moved towards his shirt pocket, then stopped as he stared at the city's former treasurer. "Since when do you smoke, Al?"

Hunstetter erupted out of his chair, pouncing across to Parnell and leaning into him threateningly. "I said kick me down a square, woman!" he snarled. "Or I'll run it up your keister 'til you start liking it."

Parnell gaped, but hastily offered him an open pack, which got snatched out of his hand and pocketed. He stared, appalled but fascinated, as Hunstetter flicked a wooden match with his fingernail and lit up. "So let's get down with it, homeboys. What kind of time am I looking at here? A dime? I'll be on the outs in four. With a six million dollar parachute waiting for me to hit the gates and pull the ripcord."

Mallory had been right, it was going to be more interesting than he could have imagined. He waved a reasonable hand. "Four years in some shithole with those animals. Maybe longer. Who knows with parole boards?"

Hunstetter shined that one on. "Not a bad bunch in here, you get to know them. Better than you fuckheads. Or that bitch I married."

"You shouldn't talk about SueAnn that way," Parnell protested. "She's a fine woman, just a little mixed-up."

Hunstetter was back in his face, looming with a glacial glare. "So you, too, eh, Brutus? I should have known. Shit, she has no standards at all."

Parnell jittered his eyes towards Mallory for help in re-directing the madman. He stepped in out of pity, "Is that a tattoo on your wrist, Al?"

Hunstetter raised his forearm to show an elaborate, Old English tat, FTW.

"Not too shabby, huh? Only cost me a pack and a half."

"Fuck The World, right?"

"Call it my new motto. Present company definitely included."

Parnell gave up, leaning back and asking querulously, "What the *hell* are you raving about?"

"You need to do better, know what I'm saying?"

"I'm afraid not," Mallory said quietly.

"Not a clue," from Parnell.

"I'll get around to clues later. If it comes to that." He took a long, theatrical drag off the cigarette, leaning back to let smoke flow from his mouth and snuff it up his nose. "Meanwhile, you guys have screwed the city for awhile: the garbage thing, contract kickbacks. You must be worth three million apiece."

"That's what I thought," Parnell told Mallory with a trace of relief, "He's gone stark, staring..."

"Shut up, bitch!" Hunstetter snapped, not only stopping Parnell's diagnosis, but blowing him back on the back legs of his chair. He took the two of them in, smirking. "You might have to sell your homes, boats, but you're good for it. It'll do. If you play it right, don't piss me off."

Mallory was really enjoying it at that point. "This is getting good. You truly surprise me, Alvin. Jail must suit you."

"It's like anything else, just vocabulary. You learn words like "solicitation to murder"."

"See?" Parnell said warily. "We should notify Doc Stillman."

"Shut up, Jerry," Mallory said agreeably. "Talk to me, Alvin. What's on your mind?"

"Oh, I don't know." Hunstetter drew it out with more cigarette technique. "A newspaper story for openers, I'd guess. Where it turns out I was innocent all along. Robbed by a mean gang, but heroically recovered the money."

Mallory broadcasted polite disappointment. "Not really front page stuff."

"You'd better hope it is. Instead of this one: Crooked Officials Frame The Treasurer And Hire A Goon To Kill Him."

"We should leave," Parnell said, urgently. "He's obviously fantasizing."

Hunstetter catapulted out of his chair again, shrugged his coveralls off his shoulders and let them fall to his feet. He showed Mallory the healing wound in his upper arm, then turned to shove his lower body, innocent of undergarments, into Parnell's face for a display of his scarred legs. "Am I fantasizing those bullet holes?" he yelled. "They know all about that March asshole, what he was. They're going to know who paid him."

Parnell knee-jerked, "You have no proof of that." Mallory started to speak but Hunstetter whirled to face him, holding up an admonishing finger. Which he thrust into his nostril.

"We got to search March's body before the cops got there, smart guys. His effects are in the proverbial safe place. Very incriminating effects, let's just say. For a muscleman assassin, he was kind of a bonehead about keeping paper around."

Mallory moved back away from the invading finger, pulled a fleecy handkerchief from his suit pocket, and offered it to Hunstetter. "You were never much at bluffing, Al."

181

"I don't have to be with this hand. You want to check and call, you go right ahead. But first you'd better count what I have left to lose, and what you do."

Abruptly, Mallory stood, briefcase in hand. "This has been interesting, Al. We'll get back to you."

You know where to find me." Hunstetter leaned back, crossing his legs and puffing smoke at the ceiling. "In the next forty-eight hours. Or I depose to Garvey and subpoena Oakley and a bunch of telephone records. What's that watchword of yours, Mal?"

Mallory stopped at the door even though Parnell was showing a marked desire to get to it and flee in confusion. He turned his full attention. "I have a watchword?"

Hunstetter mulled it, grasping for it on the tip of his tongue, then snapped his fingers. "Ironic. That's it. I-fucking-ronic."

On a second thought, he stepped over to Parnell and backhanded him hard across the face. "Oh, and Jer? You keep putting it to SueAnn and I'm going to come break it off."

The city execs were in a very subdued mood as they descended the courthouse steps and headed across the lawn. Parnell was the slower of the two, and still languished at the "denial stage" of working it out. "You realize he's out of his mind," he muttered.

But Parnell was made of sterner stuff and already to the stage where you take the damage and move on to healing. "I wish. We're going to do exactly like he said. Unless you see some other option available?"

Parnell stared at him, then pouted, "Another one of your hitmen, genius?"

"This isn't a good time to start turning on each other, Jerry. Look, we'll raise the money, replace it, grab some limelight, and move Hunstetter the hell out of here."

"With a million bucks as our personal thank you for embezzling, then blackmailing us."

"That's how it'll work out. Five for the city and one for him, is how it looks."

"Jesus Chrysler! You're talking about my fortune, Mal. My nest egg, my..."

"And where will the money go? Right back into the city coffers. Where we will have our way with it, one way or the other."

Parnell huffed and puffed over that until he reached his Volvo station wagon in the reserved spot on the street. He disarmed the alarm, stuck his key in the door, and stopped to look at Mallory. "I suppose we could just embezzle it ourselves. We could get away with it: we're smarter than that maniac geek in there."

Mallory stepped away from him, towards his charcoal Town Car. "You still believe that?"

From his cell window on the third floor, Hunstetter watched his two former colleagues scurry away. He smiled, then licked his finger and started rubbing the "tat" off his arm.

CHAPTER THIRTY-FIVE

The Mongoose wiped packing jelly off his hands with a filthy rag and reached up with a mutant torque wrench to tap an unmarked steel cylinder resting ominously on a crate. It had a dull sheen in the pulsing sunlight filtered through the camouflage net stretched over the "heavy duty" department of Mongoose's emporium of previously-owned ordinance and Flathead stared at it in mixed awe and trepidation. Not so Bogart, who was stroking the big dildo-looking tube with almost sexual delight. It looked like a ten foot long propane tank with a funnel cowl at one end and a bulbous glans-like nozzle at the other.

"Extremely rare and precious freight, dudes. You could search the world, what I'm saying." He tapped it again for emphasis, the hollow bell tone increasing Bogart's anticipation and Flatty's dread. "Mint condition RATO bottle. Unused. Duh."

"RCAT, RATO," Flathead bitched. "Why can't they just have normal names for this crap."

"You mean sensible names?" Mongoose queried condescendingly. "Like knucklehead or apehanger or iPod? What part of Rocket Assisted Take-Off don't you understand?"

Bogart vibrated with excitement, glowing as his strokes became even more erotic. "Now *that* I understand!"

"Do you really?" Mongoose examined him with an almost scientific curiosity. "You got yourself a pretty solid grasp of the implications of going from zero to Mach One in less than probably your last ever fucking heartbeat?"

"No freakin' way, Boge. Come on, man, let's get out of here. Just say No."

"Sounds fine for a pussy like you." He crawled up on the crate and straddled the one-shot, military/industrial-grade bottle rocket. He held his hands out in front of his shoulders, twisting the grips of imaginary handlebars. "Serious, Goose, what's the least you'll take for this puppy? Hey, you need any tarantulas or rattler heads?"

CHAPTER THIRTY-SIX

Two dance companions, handsome and dapper men in their fifties, leaned against the side rail, amidships on the enormous, boxy superstructure of the Coral Princess, taking a smoke break from wheeling aging widows around the opulent ballroom. They could hear the orchestra and glance through the big portholes at the lights playing on dozens of blue hair-do's inside. Relaxed in their dinner jackets, they smoked in the slight wind generated by the ocean-going monstrosity's passage through the moonlit sea and looked down the rail where Cole and Bunny Haskins were wrapped up in each other, luxuriating in the moon, sea, youth and love. Bunny was decked out to die for in a designer gown she bought on board as a move up from the Chanel number she scored in Beverly Hills before they sailed off on a cruise that would wind through the Panama Canal and return to U.S. waters short two of their most glamorous passengers. With a face and figure like that, the companions figured, there was absolutely nothing basic about the black. She looked like a movie star gone AWOL, a model in a shoot selling people on expensive perfection.

Not that there were any flies on Cole, dashing in an ice blue dinner jacket that set off his expensively barbered blond hair and went really well with his rattlesnake skin cummerbund. He beamed at her, but what she did back was beyond beams and glows. Despite his long-time, intimate and frequent knowledge of his new bride, he felt like he'd never seen her before. She combusted under the shower of moon, incandesced in the mist torn from the whitecaps and dusted by gold light from the ballroom. She'd shed her cocoon, wore the wings she was born to master; aflame with love and spirit. And only just begun.

The taller companion had eyes only for Bunny, but his stateroomie was still hung up on the old biddies they titillated. "Did you see the one that nailed me for that tango number," he asked in an injured tone. "Christ, is a free cruise really worth it?"

Still regarding Bunny, chuckling while winding a string of perfect pearls around her finger, his buddy said, "And free bar tab, don't forget. We're just human juke boxes to entertain these old dolls."

"At least we aren't allowed to sleep with them." He shuddered. "So, yeah, could be worse. We could be actual gigolos."

Down the rail Bunny hugged Cole in rapture, and he basked in it. "I take every single word back, Cole. Everything. You came through. This is the life I was born for. Slithering through the casino in silk like a Bond Girl."

Cole nodded, doting. "That casino shows me some good opportunities, now that you bring it up. I've been scoping the money trail and..."

The taller companion was drinking in the dark-haired beauty leaning over the waves. "You'd think the process of becoming a rich widow or divorcee would give these old babes a little culture. Refinement."

His pal sipped at his scotch. "Yeah, you'd think."

"Now why couldn't they be like her?" He pointed at Bunny, leaning into Cole's chest. "Just look at that. Beautiful, refined, every inch a lady.

"Every inch a red hot babe."

That got waved off in disdain. "You can buy that. But not her whole carriage of class and delicacy."

Suddenly Bunny erupted, clobbering Cole with her elegant clutch purse. He covered up, but took some stinging shots. Her admirer up the rail gaped as she basted him, yelling, "You *asshole!* I should have known!"

"Now pussycat," Cole remonstrated while trying to avoid getting clocked by her deceptively soft-looking beaded purse. "You're spoiling your Bond Girl image here."

"You're already just scheming and dying to get back to getting all shot up and hiding out! If we weren't in the middle of the ocean I'd walk out on you right this minute."

"Well, I'd have to walk right overboard with you, Buns," Cole told her while getting a good grip on her forearms. "Being stonegone crazy about you forever and ever and all."

"You'd better not even *think* of..."

"I was kidding! Just joshing you, Lil Spitfire. I got everything I need right here."

Bunny glared, then flipped to her flutter mode, moving into his arms. "Aw, baby, I know. But why do you *do* that? Spoil a wonderful time with that sordid criminal streak of yours?"

"Because I figured out socking me up gets you hot."

Bunny pulled her head back, eyes flashing, and started to retort, but Cole pulled her into a passionate kiss. She resisted a second, then melted into him as Coral Princess slid on through the night, the moonlit mist wafting them further and further away from all that old stuff back there.

The Beginning

188

More Great Books By
Linton Robinson

 Murder, romance, and baseball swirl through Mazatlan's carnival

"Pretty Woman" meets "The Godfather" in a border prison

 A fun, savage, sexy spoof on media, truth, and the American way

A rollicking soundtrack for a tale of intrigue, bad faith, and lost love.

 adoro books.com

190

Made in the USA
Lexington, KY
14 February 2013